I0712551

the LONG the SHORT and the TALL

Tales of a New American

E.P. ROSE

First Edition

Studio on 41 Press
Galisteo, New Mexico
www.galisteoliz.com

Book and cover design by Donna Brownell
Silhouettes by Elizabeth Rose

ISBN: 979-8-9869486-0-7

to Possibility

CONTENTS

the
LONG

the
SHORT

and the
TALL

FOREWORD

Writing down stories is one thing, collating them and finding a suitable title is quite another. To produce a book of short stories, the stories too random, I needed to come up with a common thread, some theme to hold each one in place. But what?

While driving, eating, sleeping, waking, all times of the day, I obsessed. Then boom, the answer dawned.

FOOL. Are you blind? The link is YOU. Every one of the stories arose from something that happened to you.

There I had it.

True. Made up. True.

I hope you, the reader, can distinguish the difference. Hmmm, maybe not, though does it really matter? Look into your own lives. TRUTH, goes the saying, is often stranger than fiction.

Is this it? All there is to life? Edging toward forty-five, almost divorced, and my grown boys partying with their friends, home-alone, I sighed. Part-time therapist, the dreary daily wait for the double decker Number 9 bus in the freezing rain to get to and back from work, stretched grey into the future. I re-read my mother's air-letter inviting me to live with her in Santa Fe New Mexico. Why now after all these years apart. I hardly knew the woman. Nor she me, for the only time we'd lived under the same roof were the three weeks I'd visited her the previous year. It wasn't that I'd wanted to be a mummy's girl, but to survive, I would need to rely on her for a while.

Should I? Shouldn't I? Hmm. Maybe I could at least give it a try. Go AWOL from the safe path my life pointed. Living with her I'd get a Green Card out of her. That at least is the one thing she could do for me, I hoped.

It's now or never, I convinced myself. I can keep on talking about it or take the plunge before I'm too old for change.

Go for it, my best friend Ann encouraged. Just last-minute nerves, she assured. Just do it. Having the chance of a new beginning is what we all would like but haven't the guts to make it happen. Again and again, she pushed me.

Hunched on the bottom stair, the phone pressed to my ear, are you sure, I pleaded. Really sure?

Still, I havered indecisive. A move to America needed courage, and courage I lacked.

If it hadn't been for that chance encounter with a stranger, I call my Butterfly Messenger, I don't think I could have severed my ties to England and stepped into the void and discovered the unknown beyond.

BUTTERFLY MESSENGER

He was a stranger. Although I do not recall his name, I still remember our one encounter more than forty years ago, at one of those appalling parties that left me wondering why in God's name I was there.

Old enough to be their father, head and shoulders above the gawky debutantes decked out in satin strapless gowns, one guest stood apart. Striking, unique, obviously, not British. Skin-tight jeans, a turquoise bolo tie dangled down his shirtfront, pointed cowboy boots, one beaded feather earring brushed his cheek, a silver plume, the other. The belt circling his hips hung low weighted by a coral-studded silver buckle, and curled about a glass of wine, his little finger flashed a silver ring. Perhaps I imagined the brimmed hat, black, sporting a horsehair hatband, because a gentleman would never wear his headgear inside a British house.

"You are not from here?" I volunteered.

"Texas. I am an escape artist."

"Really….?" I modulated my tone to disguise my skepticism.

"I was a Minister before, with my own Church and congregation. For eighteen years…" he paused. "Quite suddenly I became disillusioned, beset by grave doubts. That was it. Finish. I defrocked myself. Decided it would be hypocritical for me to stay. That very night I left and joined a circus troop. No questions asked, the ringmaster took me in and apprenticed me to his Circus Strong man. Popeye, was his name. Pinching my non-existent biceps, he shook his head. But an escape artist. I can teach you that.

Five years I traveled with Popeye in his caravan and emerged the performer I am today. That man taught me everything.

We both fell silent.

Questions I had never voiced raced to be spoken. Hypocrisy was my struggle too. Staying in a bad marriage at integrity's expense. Tied to a violent man only pretending love, I felt bound to him forever for hadn't I promised to *"love, honor and obey for as long as we both shall live?"*

"What is your view on breaking marriage vows?" I pressed him.

"A promise made by man, is not a promise made by God." His answer, firm.

The band struck up a Scottish Eightsome Reel.

As we stepped back flattening ourselves against the wall to avoid the wild fling of arms and legs, I took the moment to digest the wisdom of his words.

"What gave you courage to leave the church?"

"I summoned all my strength to blindly trust the unknown. To discover what lay across the abyss, I needed…," he paused grasping my hands to emphasize his words, "…no had to, first step into the void before I could reach the other side. There's no space for anything new to come into your life until you do."

I thanked him. Turned to leave.

"Monday, you can see my act on lunchtime television. One o'clock. Channel Two, from Birmingham. Be sure to watch," he called after me.

That Monday, home for my lunch-break, greatly skeptical, I broke my 'no-daytime-watching-television' rule. Turned on the box. Balancing a salad on my knees, I cocked half an ear towards the all-women panel discussing inane flower arrangements and outmoded etiquette.

"Next, we have special guest all the way from America……."

a woman's voice announced.

Hanging upside down, suspended from a crane, a leather-bound cocoon contorted twisted, wriggled to escape his chains. First a head emerged. Then arms, then legs. The camera zoomed to close-up. My stranger shook free, waved his limbs and smiled into the camera lens. I knew he knew I watched him. I knew his smile was for me.

Gingerly I tested my wings. It took a month and then another, for me to emerge. Once freed from marriage and my dead-end job, I became a butterfly too.

I cried of course at the airport. I don't want to leave you, my darlings. I love you, Forgive me. Emigrating is all a terrible mistake. I sobbed clinging to my two grown sons.

"Don't worry, we'll be fine, Mum," they hugged me tight and pushed me towards security. It's not like this is forever, or that we don't have a place to live."

Handing over the front-door keys to our London home, exchanging one final kiss, one last squeeze, we waved farewell.

My babies. All alone. I was a monster. How could I have done such a dreadful thing. Abandon them to fend for themselves and put my desires first. The plane nosed through the cloud belt and they and England vanished from sight.

The droning throb of the plane's engine across the pond forced me to an uneasy sleep filled with perplexing images of meandering unlit tunnels in fathomless caves. In the open air at last I found myself a flying dream I couldn't shake.

FEATHERS

"If they can, I can," I, aged eight, declared peering through the leaves. And arms flapping, launched into the air from a branch of the Cox's Pippin apple tree into which I'd clambered.

The ground hit so hard I lay flattened recovering for a slow count of five hundred.

A song thrush skimmed overhead no more than a foot above my upturned face and alighted on the branch I'd recently vacated. A flock of wing-flapping sparrows followed twittering noisily and settled in the uppermost leaves.

"Fool," I heard them deride. "No wonder she didn't fly. She forgot to wear her feathers."

No glimpse of green. Nothing similar to what I'd see back home. Approaching Albuquerque, the void my Butterfly Messenger had spoken off spread flat and brown below me. I didn't like what I saw. I wished I'd stayed in England and never chosen to move to this brown and barren place and live with the mother I barely knew. Mum? Mummy? Mother? Barbara? What to call her, I panicked.

Hello, I said spotting her, Barbara, my birth mother, at Baggage Claim.

Hello, she returned reaching for my carry-on.

In silence we walked together to her car. In silence she drove the 60 miles to her home. I dozed praying everything would be better when I woke up.

I tried, really, I did, to forge a connection based on something other than my shameful dependence on her for a place to lay my head. From the first week of my arrival, it was clear to us both long term cohabitation could never work. Two opposites, she, a neatnik, whose herbs stood alphabetically arraigned along her kitchen shelf, and me, a would-be-artist, leaving scattered snippets of card and aluminum on her floor and dining table disrupting her space. Co-habiting in such close quarters mother and daughter eyed one another warily.

I looked up Tom, an artist I'd met in London a couple of times. Wild haired, fun, eccentric, he was the perfect counter-balance to my mother's ordered ways. Nothing sexual about his intentions, over a whiskey in his favorite bar, El Farol, we listened to one another's stories and set the world aright.

TOM THE VIRGIN

When I think about memorable characters I've met, Tom comes to mind.

Tom was a virgin. That is not to say he didn't like women. He did, though they never featured in his paintings. His secret passion was to lie beside a naked 'Venus', as he called all women, worshiping with his artist's eye, without touching. His oil paintings swirled snow clouds, revealing the craggy mountains and Aspen groves he knew intimately from his weekly, solitary hikes. Sitting on the summits sketching, he captured every viewpoint with sepia ink.

"Double Rye-on-the-rocks, and a single for the lady."

Harmless. Loner. Eccentric. Talented Artist, describes Tom best.

Tom was a fun date during many a Happy Hour, before alcohol increased the volume of his voice and he became a boor. Always in a faded denim shirt, dun-colored Dockers and a brimmed felt hat to hide his balding head, his dress never varied. El Farol, a bar, the Plaza, it didn't matter where he was, live music sprung his six feet into a wild jangle of ungainly limbs. Clomping, keeping perfect time he'd dance between the tables in his clown-sized walking boots. One Bluegrass music festival he grabbed my hand and waltzed me around Santa Fe's Rodeo Ground's arena, oblivious to the cheering crowd.

Replaying roles, working his face, and gesticulating lanky arms, he repeated his stories many times. I didn't mind. Perhaps Tom's fascination with the female body began when he was nine, and shipped off to a fashionable East Coast boarding School. Searching for a sock, he discovered his locker backed onto the girl's bathroom. Working his penknife around a knot in the wood, he prized a small opening, mostly for his own use, and charged his peers five sugar-lumps a peek. One day, in his eagerness for a closer view, Tom gripped the bath's inlet pipe for a better gawk at Amy-big-tits soaping her pair of monstrous melons. Unaware, Amy leaned forward to turn off the water, inadvertently trapping his thumb between washer and tap. Tom could bear the pain no longer. He couldn't contain himself.

"Ahhh. Ahhh. Tom cried. "Amy. Amy. Quickly. Quickly. Turn the tap back on. I'm trapped." Disembodied, Tom's voice floated from the wall.

Imagining the scene, I laughed along with Tom. Oh yes. Tom could spin a goodly tale. "Did I ever tell you...?" And he'd begin

After a long night's drive to Cape Cod, Tom pulled into a café for breakfast. Finding one open, reading the menu listed on the blackboard, Tom ordered his meal. The abbreviations annoyed him. The waitress approached pen and pad in hand.

And for you, sir?

"Hm n'Chzz Snswch with Tm and Frer-Frers. Emphasizing the 'fffff' for French fries, demonstrating a rabbit face Tom bit his lower lip blowing through his teeth. And, to drink, I'll have a K-k-a-kkla. Plzzz." He added with a hiss.

The waitress fetched the manager, who threw him out. Out! At the second and the third café, it was the same.

Hungry by then, his anger mounting, Tom repeated his order for the fourth and final time. The waitress who took his order with a straight face.

"Certainly, Sir. Would you be wanting Kchup or Mstt with that? Cffee?"

I last saw Tom my friend on Santa Fe's Plaza. Limping and arthritic, his face hidden beneath the same sweat-greased hat he'd worn since we met thirty years ago, sunk beyond reach into a whiskey sodden world, he no longer remembered me.

Hmm. Live your passion, the command had jumped from the self-help book. *Not so easy,* I thought. *I missed my children, my friends and family, and my independence. Suddenly a home-less, unemployed, middle aged, spinster daugh-ter living with her mother earning chump change teaching at a local pre-school was not the new image I'd imagined. A failure, I belonged nowhere. No fairy godmother in sight to wave her magic wand and change my life.*

Cooped up at my mother's, I read of Llorona, Chupacabra... learned of Curanderas, Penitentes, Pilgrimas and cures of healing sand. I heard tales of folk lore and the Day of the Dead.

I stood with the crowd to watch Zozobra burn. I held my breath as Pueblo dancers danced for rain to the beat of a drum. Kachina Dolls, Dream Catchers... my mind spun. I wanted to know the culture I'd chosen to live in. I wanted to write a folk story of my own. The New Mexican awarded me second place in their Christmas writing com-petition with a cheque for fifty dollars.

TOO OLD...MY FIRST ENGLISH CHRISTMAS

The first ever Christmas I remember in England, and too young to know better, I foolishly announced I no longer believed in Father Christmas as we English call him. Not Santa, as he's more frequently known today in America.

Not yet eight, my brother aged four, we were only one year off the ship from India. Living way out in the countryside of Devonshire, a county of moors and windswept hills, my brother and I shared home with between a fluctuating gaggle of between five and seventeen of us children. A sort of paying orphanage, "Thornworthy," a large, rambling English Country House housed the offspring of us children whose parents' work took them overseas for years at a time. Abandoned some might say, and not wanting to be hampered, my father handed us into an Auntie Baba's care and sailed for Ethiopia.

Auntie Baba ruled with a slipper and prayers loving us the best way she knew. Scared as we were of her, we latched onto her mother figure to give us some sense of belonging.

With so many of us, life in the Victorian house was a bit like living the nursery rhyme, *The old woman who lived in a shoe, who had so many children she didn't know what to do.*

Known as the bad winter of '47, snow fell darkening the windows of Thornworthy's ground floor, sealing the doors with deep drifts as the Himalayan snowfall I remembered, the winter I'd spent in Gulmarg, Kashmir.

Marooned for almost two whole months, Auntie Baba stitched

woolen scarves into long-tailed pixie hats and sent us out into the cold wearing only fingerless gloves. Isolated from the nearest village, we children were volunteered into dragging toboggans over two miles each way, to collect our bread and groceries from the closest drop off point the other side of a steep hill.

Tramping and laughing at ourselves as we sank in the deep snow, my friends and I made forays into the winter wonderland to snip great armfuls of dark green prickly holly leaves laden with shiny red berries peeking from the tops of the hedgerows, and sticky boughs of white mistletoe and olive we found eye-level embedded into a branch of a hollow oak tree in Homeclose field. I still remember the tinkling sound of icy-encrusted leaves when they clanged together.

As Christmas drew closer our preparations for the festival intensified. Divided into groups, one feverishly cutting gaily-colored paper into strips, one stirring pots of flour and water into a gooey paste, another looping the sticky strips to long paper chains till their coiled heaps lay in untidy piles on the green lino of the playroom floor. Adults teetered on chairs stringing the colored chains from corner to corner, ceiling light too wall, till every downstairs room was festooned with color. Never mind the dangerous weight of mistletoe and holly too close to hot light fixtures, Thornworthy transformed into a magical castle.

I am telling you all this because in the midst of this activity, a lull fell. So engrossed were we with the serious job in hand, I took it upon myself to very clearly, and very loudly announce, I am too old now to believe in Father Christmas any more.

Didn't stop me though on Christmas Eve from hanging up my knee sock on the metal rail at the end of my bed that night along with all the other children in my dorm. Or from the excitement of discovering a red balloon tied to my bulging sock topped with a cracker jutting from the opening; the mysterious appearance of a silver foil covered tangerine in the toe, then nuts and sweets, a paper trumpet, a pencil, a plastic miniature charm and best of all a bag of glass marbles.

"Father Christmas must have come with his boots off," my friends exclaimed awed, for not one of us had seen or heard him.

I kept my mouth tight shut as by then, though not quite so not believing as before, I wasn't quite believing either.

I don't remember Christmas lunch itself, but it was after we had eaten and sitting around the fifteen-foot-long oblong table still wearing our paper crowns from the pulled and discarded Christmas Crackers, and playing a rowdy hand game of Up Jenkins with silver three-penny bits and farthings, and having a rare good time and a laugh, that I heard them—BELLS.

"Shhh...Children," Baba called us to silence cupping an ear with one hand. "LISTEN. Sleigh bells. Can you hear them?"

Tinkle. Tinkle. Louder by the second, the unmistakable sound of bells. God's truth, every one of us could hear them. We became ever so quiet, as with eyes wide and round as shillings, the bells drew closer.

Pushing back our chairs we dashed crowding to the window to peer into the dusk of grey, winter sky. No sign of him out there.

"He must already be over our chimney," Baba announced "Hurry children, let's go into the Smoking Room and see if he's arrived."

Normally taboo, we children were rarely allowed into the hallowed environs of the smoking room, not because of smoking, but because the room was reserved for the cleaning and nurse maids.

The drawn maroon velvet curtains left just enough outside light to make out shadowy shapes. As we pushed and shoved each other to be the first inside, Baba called out excitedly shushing us "Shhh... I think he's in the chimney."

The hairs on the back of my neck stood up and my legs started to tremble, I remember, for to my horror and terror little flakes of soot began falling into the fireplace, and from inside the chimney breast came the faintest, then stronger and stronger scratch, scratching.

Then, horror. One black toe cap of a boot appeared, then a second followed by red trousered legs swinging back and forth until with a plump Father Christmas dropped into the fireplace pulling down a bulky sack behind him from the chimney. White beard and eyebrows, the reddest cheeks and nose just like all the pictures of him I had seen. Father Christmas. He was real!

All us children had been frightened seeing soot raining into the fireplace and had even tried to run away fearful of what was scrabbling in our chimney. Alan, the youngest of us, even screamed. Luckily, there was no fire laid and burning in the grate that day.

Without a "Ho. Ho. Ho." But in a trembly, old sort of voice, he called to us "Me-rry Chri-st-mas- chil-dren. Me-rry Chri-st-mas- to- you- all." Then he waved, beckoning. Just a little bit less scared by then, we waved shyly back too surprised to speak.

It was then that he asked a question that almost made my stomach drop and my heart stop dead.

"Ha-ve-all—the-chil-dren—been-g-o-od?"

Baba turned, gazing at each one of us, one by one, severe and unsmiling.

Recent dreadful deeds came vividly to mind: I'd crawled into the attic and fallen through the ceiling: I'd try to fly, stealing one of Baba's umbrellas and had turned the spokes inside out: Worst of all, I had said out loud that I did not believe in him, in Father Christmas. I held my breath.

Reaching into his sack, he pulled out a green and red covered package and handed it over to Baba. Smiling now, checking the label, she called out a name before handing it back to Father Christmas. "Jennifer." He repeated, "Merry Christmas! " And beckoned her to come close and take her present. "Peter." It was his turn." Anna." " Norman." "Guy." Then my brother Mike and so on and on. The sack became floppier as it emptied.

"What about me? Had I been too naughty? Oh please, I promise to be good. I'll be a good girl." I said to myself over and over again.

Just as I was ready to burst into tears, I heard

"Is there an Elizabeth here?"

He hadn't forgotten me. I moved shyly to shake his hand and accept my present, the very last package. I don't recall what it was that he brought me, but whatever it was did not matter.

After distributing a mince-pie and a chocolate each, it was time for Father Christmas to leave. Baba escorted him out through the kitchen and back lobby to his sleigh.

"It's parked outside the back door," Baba said telling us watch from the window and wait where we were until we heard his sleigh bells."

Jingle, tinkle. Bells.

In one mighty swoop and a rush seventeen faces crowded the window staring up into the black starless sky.

Was that a speck of light I saw? In it Father Christmas shaking the reins of his sleigh? Was that him geeing his six reindeer to fly ever higher up and up away into the sky? His voice I heard fading with a Ho. Ho. Ho.

Oh yes, I do believe in Father Christmas again.

*E*ncouraged I submitted a Christmas story to the monthly competition run by the Southwest Writers I'd recently joined. Wow. Honorable Mention. I stared at the ornate certificate that fell from the envelope. Over the years a dozen or more certificates from my writing have accumulated in my folder marked Contests.

ANNA
A WINTERS TALE

Anna pushed her feet into her bedroom slippers, wrapped her dressing gown tight, and reached for her bedside clock.

"Fall back. Spring forward."

She turned the tiny hands all the way around the face from six to five. No larger than a pocket watch, the silver clock had stood on her mother's dressing table all of Anna's childhood. Now it was hers. She glanced at the photo on the nightstand, reminding herself of her mother's face and sighed. Daylight savings…winter, already?

Anna lifted the porcelain kitchen clock down onto the table from the blue wooden shelf. It read ten past six. Delicately painted with cornflowers, it matched the pair of old-fashioned china plates displayed on either side.

"Remember, Anna. Hands clockwise." Father spoke clearly in her head. Winding the clocks had become a weekly ritual they enjoyed together while mother was dressing in her Sunday Best, and fussing over which hat to wear to Church.

"Does this look good, Carlito?" Mother coo-ed from their bedroom. "Or do you prefer this one?"

If he chose the blue, she chose the brown. While they were both alive, the game was the same each Sunday, until mother indicated she'd made her final choice by pushing a steel hatpin firmly into place.

Anna pulled out the stop on the backside of the clock and twisted it between her forefinger and thumb till it stiffened.

"Careful, Anna, or you'll over-wind."

Remembering father's words, Anna paused holding the time-piece to her ear, listening to its barely audible tick. Twenty past five. No point going back to bed. The warm patch under her eiderdown would be long cold. She filled the kettle, placed it on the burner and shuffled to her bedroom to get dressed.

When the kettle's whistle summoned her to the kitchen, she poured a splash of boiling water into the brown Denby teapot mother brought from England when she was eighteen.

"First warm the pot." Now it was mother's voice that spoke from the grave.

"One heaped teaspoon per person, one for the pot."

While the tea brewed, she pushed open the parlor door and shivered. The room remained chilly until late afternoon.

Anna wrinkled her nose at the heavy oak domed clock standing on its fake brass feet. God only knows why father loved it so. Mother had sniffed her disapproval when he brought it home and placed it proudly on her mantle.

"Happy birthday, Maggie dear. I hope you like it," he'd smiled producing her gift from behind his back.

And so the ugly thing sat loudly ticking in the empty room for almost fifty years.

Keeping it level, Anna slid it carefully around and pried off the metal back. Inserting the key, she wound the movement first, then the chime, before facing the clock back into room. She kept exactly to that order.

"You'll put its timing out. Clocks are very sensitive, Anna."

"Yes, yes father, every week you tell me," she mocked impatiently to herself.

Anna opened the glass face. Pointing her right forefinger, she forwarded the hour hand to six, to seven counting the hours' chimes under her breath, then on again to eight, to nine, to ten, all the way round till at last the clock struck five.

"That's a good job done."

She glanced outside at the turkey vultures circling the Bosque. The cottonwoods blazed yellow.

"Late this year, they are. Winter will be hard, see if I'm not right."

She spoke to nobody in particular.

To celebrate the changing season, Anna followed her mother's tradition by cooking a pot of beans.

"A warming dish to welcome winter."

Anna chose black beans, remembering to soak them in a saucepan overnight with a pinch of bi-carbonate as mother showed her.

"Stops gas." She'd nod tapping her belly and winking.

As Anna drained the swollen beans under running water, one bean caught her attention. It had grown a long tendril root, and a tiny folded green-beginnings of a leaf the opposite end.

"Curious. Thinks it's spring."

Anna fished it out, laid it on a paper towel, cut one scoop from an egg box in her fridge and filled it with soil skimmed from one of her potted geraniums.

"Perfect." and placed it on the table by the window.

"Now I'll see what you are made of."

She hurriedly ate a slice of thickly buttered toast and marmalade with her tea before tackling the beans.

Unfolding her mother's hand written recipe she smoothed its stained and faded linen paper, and although she knew it by heart, checked off each ingredient. Cheered, tying on her apron, she set herself to such a frenzy of chopping, slicing and adding pinches of this and that, she made herself quite out of breath.

"I'd better hurry." she addressed the plant.

Like mother, she fussed in front of the looking glass alternating hats as she readied for Church. The day was glorious and she chose her 'yellow-felt' to match the autumn leaves in the Bosque.

"Morning, Miss Anna."

Her neighbor Sam, looked up from forking his front flowerbed by the gate. Five years ago, it was, his family moved in. Young and noisy, they were friendly enough, but not people to drop by unannounced, like the old days. As her friends died or moved away, new folk had nudged out the old, house by house.

When she returned from Church, she took off her Sunday Best and she was startled to see the plant had sprouted a good half inch. Anna ate a bowl of beans eyeing it warily.

"A larger pot for you, my dear."

October left in a mighty windstorm taking all the color from the leaves and the turkey vultures with it. By Thanksgiving the plant stood one foot proud. Anna had already repotted it twice. The first time she used the tin from the plum-cake her nephew sent from Australia. Each year his parcel arrived early. She never waited for Christmas Day to cut into it.

Only two weeks later her pine tree, for it was clear now what the plant was, needed something larger. This time, Anna placed a small piece of bacon fat and a copper penny at the bottom of the pot before covering both with good earth.

Mrs. Jenkins from Meals on Wheels, clearly thunderstruck, joked every time she visited on her deliveries.

"My." She exclaimed. "You feeding it my dinners, Anna dearie?"

Anna didn't mention the copper penny or the bacon fat, or how she crooned and spoke to it during mealtimes at their shared table.

"Well, my beauty, any plans today?" or, "A little drop of water, perhaps?"

She never got a real answer, though she swore the pine tree

nodded.

Christmas Eve descended dark and cold. Anna drew the curtains and locked the front door early. Setting her jewelry box on the table, Anna announced to the pine,

"You are my precious Christmas Tree."

Saving a silver star for the top, she clipped her prettiest earrings onto the branches, spiraled a silver chain and her broken string of pearls up and around, then finished up nicely covering the branches with fluffed cotton wool.

"There you are my beauty," Anna, beamed stepping back to admire her handiwork. "…all ready for tomorrow."

"Must have left the kitchen lights on."

Anna stumbled out of bed and gasped as she opened the door. The tree glowed, every piece of jewelry a twinkling light, and sprinkled around its base, what at first she assumed were pinon shells, were her favorite chocolate almonds.

Anna lowered herself into her chair lost in wonder and fell asleep by the last glow of the fire to an angelic voice singing,

"It came upon a midnight clear…"

Should. Should. I knew I should be more grateful to my mother for I could see she found my living with her as difficult as I did living with her. As an émigré I had it easy...food, a home, and yet I still hadn't found a way to fully support myself. Depressed, I thought back to Uncle Bunny, the guardian who sheltered me throughout my childhood who ran away from home; the first time with his Grandmama when he was only four, then again for good when he came of age at eighteen. Uncle Bunny did it. He managed to forge a life for himself in Burma without anybody's help, and return to England with a fortune in his pocket. If an eighteen-year-old could overcome such hurdles overseas, then surely, I could make it in a country where people spoke as I did.

UNCLE BUNNY

Sir Edmund Bernard Pratt. A grand name for such a tiny man. Uncle Bunny, I called him. Small in stature, I thought him mighty.

One of twins, weighing in at two and a half pounds, he and twin sister spent their first two months of life struggling to survive swaddled inside one of their father's sheepskin slippers before a coal fire.

Normally, not much for chatter, dinner over, his plate pushed aside, Uncle Bunny spun his tales. Brandy in hand and puffing on his pipe, leaning back in his chair Uncle Bunny held me spellbound.

"You didn't...?" At ten years old, I shivered as he related an act of boldness or past adventure, or the time he quelled a rioting crowd on his own.

"Tell me about how you ran away. Pleee-ase," I egged him on.

"It was Granny's idea," Uncle Bunny, began. Tobacco pipe in mouth inhaled long and deep. "Granny and I decided to run away. We both disliked my father intensely and had our own reasons to escape father's iron hand. One afternoon she called me to her."

I was not yet five and she, the oldest of old ladies, confined to a bath chair was my best friend. I need your help, my Granny whispered checking she couldn't be overheard. I want to run away. Come with me and we'll run away together. Her decision was spur of the moment. Let's go, she said, and so we did. Right then.

Pushing her bath chair on the gravel was a little hard for me at first, but luck was on our side. Once the length of the garden path was behind us, and I got her wheel chair to the main gate, a gentle slope took charge and rolled us along at a great lick. Using her free hand to keep hold of her hat, Granny urged me on excitedly pointing with her cane and calls of "Onward. Onward. That's the stuff, Bunny, Tally-ho." We had barely traveled two miles along the high-walled leafy country lane in the direction of the village, when, red in the face and shouting horribly, father caught up with us in his carriage.

"Halt. This very minute. I forbid you to move another inch. Where the devil do you imagine you are going?" He cracked his whip menacingly making both the horses and me twitch.

"Get in Hugh, you naughty boy. NOW. Shame on you Mother," he barked, and ordered two servants to force her into the carriage. Her bath chair strapped to the Dickie at the back, they lifted her unceremoniously onto the seat ignoring Granny's, "How dare you touch me, you insolent man." Being only four and small for my size, my foot wouldn't reach the Brougham's high step, when suddenly an iron grip clamped me about the waist and practically threw me in. Father kept silent on the drive home, his lips set tightly closed as the lid of his snuffbox. I don't know what father said to Granny, but my punishment was to be sent to bed, locked into my room for the rest of the day with bread and water for my supper. Mother wept outside my door. I could hear her, but father's orders stood. Granny abandoned me the same year. Gone to the bosom of our Great Redeemer in heaven. Mother said. I remember being cross Granny left me behind and not taken me with her.

By the time I was a lad of about ten we were at war, father and I. I never knew why or what he was looking for, but he took to searching my room, my private domain, whenever I was out, everything just a little out of place from how I had left things. I knew it was father. I was sure. I saw the way he looked at me as if he hoped to catch me out, read my thoughts. Just as well he couldn't see what I was plotting, dreaming up the perfect pay back.

One cold November day, before leaving the house for school, I filled my china washbasin from its matching water jug and soaked my large sea-sponge with as much icy water as it could hold, then carefully balanced its dripping mass on the top of my bedroom door and pulled it almost closed, leaving it ever so slightly ajar.

My schoolwork suffered that day, and Miss Jenson whacked six painful stripes across my open palm. I didn't mind too much, with each stroke of the cane, I was picturing, *Splat! Splat!* And father's face as the sodden sponge fell right onto his balding pate when began his snooping in my room.

Although I never had the pleasure of actually seeing the fruits of my joke, I laughed myself silly just knowing I had scored. He knew that I knew that he knew it was me who paid him back. His spying stopped, though not before he trumped up some reason to thrash my wickedness out of me. But it was well worth the pain of father's strap across my backside and legs.

Hatching my plan of escape, I lay in wait determined to run away again. This time forever. Over the summer before I turned eighteen, I invented reasons to go to town and secretly visit my father's tailor. Using my father's account, I ordered three tropical suits, three pairs of casual slacks, a navy-blue blazer with brass buttons, and six shirts without paying a penny. And at the tailor's suggestion, I picked out a fine Panama straw hat. It added several inches to my height. The perfect gentleman if I might say so, Sir, the tailor smiled. Packed, a letter confirming a job-offer of a Bank-clerk's position in Rangoon, Burma, and a one-way passage booked in steerage on a cargo steamer in my pocket, that very night I made my escape and sailed to India with nothing but the unpaid-for set of tropical clothes I charged secretly to father's account. I did pay him back in full years later after I had made my fortune.

On the ship, one passenger took a sudden liking to me. Middle-aged, and twice my size, her constant attentions pestered me. With so few passengers on board, it was difficult to escape her advances. I'd had enough. Knowing a skylight opened from the upper deck onto her first-class cabin, I dropped the ship's cat through the opening landing it directly on her bunk while she was resting. You never heard such yowls and shrieks. What a commotion. She must have suspected who the culprit was for she ignored me the rest of the voyage. Now, who do you think the Bank Manager's wife turned out to be...? She had me sacked within the week. Good thing as it turned out. The Hong Kong bank offered me a better job with better pay."

From those desperate beginnings, Uncle Bunny moved to India and rose through the ranks to become Chairman of an International company based in Calcutta for twenty years. Reposted to head office in London, he eventually retired and died in England.

It was a cold November day, I remember, the last time I saw Uncle Bunny.

"Oh good. Just in time. Sir Bernard asked to be awake for you. Hurry, the effect of the injection won't last long," his doctor greeted ushering me to his bedside.

As I pushed open the oak paneled door of his dressing room, he turned his head and smiled, holding his skeletal hand towards me.

"Oh. Uncle Bunny, I'm so sorry," I half sobbed.

Propped on starched linen pillows, dressed in blue monogrammed pyjamas, wearing his habitual kerchief knotted loosely around his neck, the paisley eiderdown gave no hint of the body it covered. At eighty-nine, his head still sprouted hair, and though sallow from years spent in India, his skin, still smooth, looked barely wrinkled.

"Your pendant …. It's gone." Horrified, I cried, instantly noticing.

"Nurse took it off," he whispered.

For thirty years, the talisman never once left his neck, not since the time in Calcutta, his Bearer of twenty-years hung the white sapphire about his neck with the blessing, to keep you safe, wear this and no harm will come.

His eyes pointed to the dresser. Quickly searching, I found the pendant partly hidden beneath his pair of silver-backed hair-brushes, and clasped it back around his neck. Searching with his hand, he clutched the shining jewel, smiled, then closed his eyes never to re-awake.

I sobbed at his funeral four days later.

Fifty years have flown. Today, I hold his crystal paperweight, see him still, and hear his tales.

I have an idea my mother announced over her cocktail one evening. I've decided to build a casita in the garden...for you to live in rent free for my lifetime in exchange for help when I need it. You would have a studio. I would get back my life. Both of us smiled the day I moved into the casita.

The exchange worked. I ran her errands, drove her to appointments, shared Wheel of Fortune and her cocktail hour.

I'd been my mother's not so willing companion for almost a year when the phone rang. My best friend in England was dead. Chatting happily one minute, thrown from the car, the next, her life extinguished, the message it was time to focus on my sculpture, flashed into my mind. Life was short. I got that. I flew to London.

I buried my friend and on my return to Santa Fe, abandoned my teaching. I picked up a chisel, borrowed money to buy a plasma cutter, and stared at my first sheet of steel. Non-verbal communication, verbal communication, not so different to Speech Pathology after all, I'd speak through my work. A small gallery on Santa Fe's world renowned Canyon Road accepted my first pieces. I stared at my first cheque.

It wasn't until then, the moment I decided, the moment I stepped into the void that it happened, my Butterfly Messenger's message came true.

For the first time answer I am a sculptor, if anyone asked ...and what do you do?

SANDRA

She was smiling when they found her bedded among the wheat stalks, eyes fixed open in surprise. Not a mark on her face, so lovely she looked, arms and fingers spread on the golden earth, her hair flamed by the setting sun. When I learned of the crash, how she died, her neck broken, I imagined her an angel flying through the window, the blue cotton of her frock, flapping wings.

Sandra, died in that road accident while holidaying in Spain. On wakeful nights this past month, I think of her, my best friend. My dearest English friend.

Tragic. So young. So Beautiful. At least she didn't suffer. I let the mourners' whispered remarks drift, not saying anything.

"At least that's true," I thought, "she would never have to see an old woman's face stare back at her from the mirror."

It wasn't possible to imagine Sandra any way but glamorous. Slackening skin and creeping lines of age were not for Sandra. Growing old was not an option for my beautiful friend. I wondered what curve her life might have taken if she'd been born plain, if her father had survived the war and not left her mother a widow, so lonely, she quickly swore till death do us part to a Texan.

Sandra fed on men's lust for her body as if to make up for her own lack of desire. *But they wanted it,* she answered me one day when I asked her if she'd really enjoyed sex with three different men in the same day.

Since I met her, her promiscuity had been a puzzle to me. *And you, you're such a prude,* she would laugh. Both of us British, both from broken homes, both of us brought up in India, both living in Santa Fe New Mexico, no surprise she and I became such fast friends.

Who was I to judge her after…after she confided her story; those years of early childhood from four to twelve, those years she lived in India, the string of bastards, beginning with her American stepfather who took advantage of her innocence, couldn't keep his fingers from creeping under her knicker-leg-elastic when neither her mother or Ayah, were around.

"My new daddy sat beside me on the settee of our bungalow and read me books. I liked his arm stroking mine, so it was partly my fault that he….," Sandra faltered unable to say the word.

Looking over at her hunched figure I waited for her to continue. Not yet dawn, crouched together in my car, a thermos of coffee to warm us, we talked and shared our secrets over the many long hours of waiting for the market to open so we could stall-out our nick-nacks and make enough money to buy enough groceries for the weekend. Enough to feed her four, and my two boys.

"Mummy and I wore matching cotton dresses," Sandra continued. "Her hem, knee length. Mine six inches shorter, halfway up my thigh. "My beauties, just look at the two of you," Sandra remembers her step-daddy saying, sliding his arm around her waist.

"Liquid is a must in the heat, and water is for frogs." Laughing at her own joke, her mother clapped her hands demanding the bearer to add a dash of vodka to her breakfast orange juice. I'm living in a blasted furnace. Too hot to move, Piggy darling." When booze blurred Mummy's world, she blew me a kiss goodnight with the hand fanning herself—the hand not clutching her second evening peg of G'n'T. "Do go upstairs and say goodnight to Piggy for me will you, Teddy, dear boy," she'd plead.

When he came into my room, I put my arms round his neck, and when he kissed my cheek, I hugged and kissed him back. *You don't smell the same as Mummy.* I remember saying as the nightly training how to satisfy his desire began. If mother suspected, she didn't say a thing.

Mother un-seeing, I became a shadow in my mother's haze. An irritating food crumb to brush from her lap. When I turned ten and a half and began my period, she shooed me from her to an English boarding school. I belonged to no person, no country. Not to England, to America, not to India. Mummy faded. Became as ornamental as a plumped cushion on the cane armchair after Teddy's job took us to India.

By the chance mix of my mother and father's genes, the features of my face and body aligned themselves so prettily I grew up believing I was beautiful. Though when the midwife handed mother the tight wrapped cocoon showing only my closed eyes, squashed nose and flared nostrils she cried out, "God. I've birthed a piglet," to everyone who came to oooh and ahhh at her firstborn—me. "You came out bald, pink and wrinkled, darling. But look at you now, Piggy."

I could see from her smile Mother had been really proud, really loved me, her darling baby.

During those first weeks of life, my screwed-up features opened from a rosebud to a rose, my nose grew pert, and fine blonde hairs tufted my scalp.

These memories I hold close—the birth story's frequent repetition, strangers touching, stroking my cheek, my head, the words they murmured, lovely child, so pretty, a real beauty, a heartbreaker that one. I loved the warm feeling inside when Mother called me by nickname, Piggy. I was still her darling then. Before Teddy moved in with us and spoiled it all. I scattered marigold and gardenia petals from a basket at Mummy's wedding to my new step-dad. "You'll soon love him, Piggy. And he'll love you like your dead daddy used to do." Mummy kissed me, but her eyes looked over my head at something I couldn't see.

"You see I grew up vain. I played to my audience, loving the attention. I watched them watching me. Them liking it when I licked my lips as mother did, and when I pushed out my chest wishing them, the boobies I didn't yet have. So, it was my fault men touched me." Sandra paused.

I didn't interrupt. I pictured us before dawn, crouched together in my car, a thermos of coffee to warm us, we talked and shared our secrets over the many long hours of waiting for the market to open.

Now she had died.

Poor Sandra. Poor sad little girl. My poor lonely friend, giving her body to any man for loveless sex a fair exchange, not for her own pleasure, but for the brief illusion of being truly loved.

I wiped my hand across my face, stopped a stream of tears, and turned my focus back to Sandra's wake, to what the lover she'd taken with her on that fatal trip to Spain was telling me.

"The sun was in my eyes and I …." Wiping his nose with the back of his hand, he sniveled unable to continue.

Averting my gaze, disgusted, I listened unable to bring myself to comfort him—the man who'd caused her death. I imagined the sun's blinding rays beaming parallel to the hardtop's surface, the tear and scrunch of metal, Sandra's screams, the sudden slam of brakes, and the strumming of the guitar music from the car's radio still playing in the stillness of the wheels spinning. I heard the silence, pictured the scene, saw Sandra's eight-year-old son jerked back to consciousness to the horror of the bicycle's tangled wheels, its embedded spokes, the cyclist's animal moan, the blood pool, and then the panic finding the passenger door ajar.

His mother missing.

"Don't forget your seatbelt," Sandra's latest amour, Greg, reminded as he clicked his seatbelt in position.

"Please Mum." Sandra's son begged, already strapped in.

Greg had reached across her pulling on the belt strap, and running his hand across the light cotton of her skirt over her thigh set her giggling. But she tossed the belt-buckle away, he continued. "I need to be free," she'd laughed. Ironic, looking back.

Setting off along the narrow road between the stubble of the wheat field and the stone wall, Sandra tipped her head partly out of the open passenger window to allow the wind to snatch at her hair.

"I'm alive. I'm alive," she sang. Perhaps her last words on earth.

Standing at the graveside on plastic grass, her grave had yawned so deep, so black, I hated knowing she lay down there in the dark alone.

"Here, Sandra. A little piece of New Mexico…" and I let a handful of the desert soil she so loved and a sprig of pinon and juniper I'd brought with me all the way from Santa Fe, sprinkle her coffin.

"So, you'll feel at home," I whispered.

Summiting Hermit's 11,000-foot peak one Wednesday with my hiking friends, I paused to catch my breath and heard a Golden Eagle's cry echo from the depths below the tree line, triumphant, calling, calling. Surveying the view spread around and about me as I searched for him and I saw the monsoon thunder clouds gathered along the horizon melt into the thin air, disappear before my eyes. And as they vanished, the child in India I'd kept hidden since aged five slipped her hand in mine and stood beside me.

Now, now, the eagle screamed overhead.

My best friend gone, I had no time to waste.

I transferred my work to a downtown Co-op gallery with its better walk-in traffic, and dollars, real greenbacks, began to flow into my pocket. I paid tax. Now I as a person, needed to change. In a town where aura balancing, past lives, aliens, underground bases, UFOs, chakras and the end of the age of Aquarius were the norm, nobody cared whether I used the correct knife and fork, or wore what clothes to what occasion, as British society demanded.

Since arriving in New Mexico I experimented with alternative therapies and discovered acupuncture.

I'd like to trade one of your sculptures in payment for the treatments I've given you, my friend and acupuncture therapist suggested.

"Great idea," I agreed without a second thought.

A FAIR TRADE

"How about a trade?" My acupuncturist inquired, pulling the last needle from the crown of my head.

"Yes," I responded without thinking, my brain addled by the probe. As a second rung sculptor struggling to break into in Santa Fe's Art scene, money always short, I owed her for a dozen sessions.

"I need three hundred floor tiles brought from Juarez by next week for the new extension so they can be laid in time for Christmas. I've a borrowed my yardman's flatbed. All I need is a driver. It's about a six-hour drive. All expenses paid. Are you on?" She asked removing a long needle from my head and dabbing at a drop of blood with a cotton ball. "Pretty fair exchange, don't you agree?"

"Have you seen much of New Mexico, yet?" I asked a photographer friend, Susan, at a gallery opening.

"I need to drive across the border into Mexico within the next couple of days and wondered if you'd be my co-driver? We can go the back way via the Petroglyphs at Three Rivers Park and White Sands National Monument, have a margarita-stop at The Double Eagle in La Mesilla where Billy-the-Kid had a shoot-out, before spending the night in El Paso's Historic district. Make it fun."

A new arrival to the City Different artist, I hoped the trip would entice her.

"You sound like a tourist guide." She laughed. "When do we leave?"

It was the first week in December, the days, cold, the sky, ice-blue. We'd leave the following day.

"The truck's an oil-guzzler, so keep topping-up. Oh, and by the way, first gear is shot. You have to start in second gear." My acupuncturist dropped the information, casually, glancing at me sideways when I went to pick it up. "Don't worry. It's no problem," she lied.

I stared aghast at the truck's beat-up metallic once blue body-paint and cracked windscreen, warily eying its long wooden flat-bed. I had once driven a V.W. bus for a friend, but never anything that large.

"You'll be fine." The acupuncturist added, noticing my horri-fied expression. "Here. Take the key."

Reaching up to the cab, I hauled myself into the cab, adjusted the seat and gingerly set off for my boyfriend's home in Galisteo, a small village about twenty miles south of Santa Fe.

Rising before dawn, I made coffee, filled a thermos, and study-ing the map, traced my finger along State Roads 41, 64, 70…. *'Cuckoo. Cuckoo. Cuckoo.* Six times, the maddening bird sprung through the wooden doors of the Swiss clock in his kitchen reminding me Susan was late.

"Said she'd be here by six." I muttered glancing at the time. "I hope to God she's on her way."

I opened the back door and peered anxiously into the dark. Horror. A thin layer of snow covered every pinon tree, every cholla, the truck, and the ground. At that moment, Susan's head-lights pierced the dark as she swung into the driveway. To my relief, the headlight beam showed the snow was no longer falling.

"I'm here." Susan said gaily.

Lurching in second gear I negotiated the flatbed out of the driveway. Dark tracks trailed behind us where its tires had bit-ten through the white. Gathering speed, the truck coasted down the hill past the Cemetery towards the village church to join

Highway 41.

"Too fast. The truck's a back-wheel drive. Whatever you do, don't brake," Susan shouted over the engine's whine.

"What did you say?" Too late I understood, as I slammed the brakes spinning the truck 360 degrees before it stopped facing back up the hill we'd just come down. Weighted with our near disaster for the next eight miles quiet clouded the cab.

As we cruised towards Comanche gap beyond Galisteo, the pink-tinged in the rising sun, the rolling silhouette of Cero Pelon emerged from the dawn's mist. Discarnate, the mountain hung suspended above the grass filled basin.

"Photo Op," Susan gasped, and our gloom dispelled.

"Photo Op," she shouted. Every few miles it seemed something magical caught our eye.

"Look. Look. Look," we'd both yell, and I'd brake to a shuddering to a halt in the emptiness of a lonely road. Out she jumped with her camera, focus the lens and shoot.

"Great shot," she'd sigh clambering back in. "More like it. Now I'm having fun."

The small New Mexican villages of Stanley, Moriarty, and Estancia, slipped past un-noticed.

Two hours into the journey on the approach to Cedar Grove where the road stretched ruler-straight, wet snowflakes began splattering the cracked windscreen.

"That's all we need," I cursed, feeling for the truck's wiper switch.

The blades squeaked right to left a couple of arcs, then froze angled awkwardly across the glass. With just a couple of miles to the little town ahead, Susan leaned out of the window and using her gloves frantically wiped open a small viewing hole that disappeared as fast as it was cleared. Somehow, just enough to keep driving, we limped into Corona's only gas station to wait out the storm.

While Susan propped the hood open with both hands, I clambered onto the bumper to check the guzzler's oil. Bending dangerously over the radiator and into the engine, I had to first dislodge a packrat's nest of prickly cholla in order to reach the dipstick and feed in a quart then another and another..

Sheltered in the warmth of the cab, our hands cupped round mugs of hot coffee we peered up at the sky assessing our situation. "We can't be that feeble," we both agreed. "Give up after we've made it this far."

"I'm game to keep going, but not if it keeps snowing." Susan declared.

"Let's give it to Carrizozo before we decide. It's bound to be warmer further south."

As if in agreement, the engine almost purred, a patch of grey-blue appeared, and my driving-butterflies finally quieted. We spent the next sixty miles marveling at the vastness of the land with its isolated ranches and groves of water-starved cottonwoods.

"Think of the pioneers struggling to survive out here. Look how sad," I commented, pointing out a forlorn windmill. Sentinel to a still-standing chimneybreast, sails motionless, it stood beside the blackened fireplace and sad heap of crumbled adobe. Unlike the defeated homesteaders, the gnarled trees, planted so long ago, still clung to life.

"Antelope. Look." Rolling down the windows and pulling onto the verge, I silenced the engine. "One, two, three…fifteen," we whispered counting. Our breath steamed white into the December air.

Curious as we were, the grazing herd lifted their dainty heads return our gaze. We must have stared at one another for a full five minutes. Then slowly, Susan lifted her zoom lens and aimed,. With a flash of their white rumps, the herd wheeled north leaping and springing high over the tall grasses headed for a distant patch of cholla.

"Well your zoom does look like a gun."

Two hours further on, our country road joined the main truckers' highway halfway to the distant border, containers and open trucks stacked with junk cars barreled down the highway, we spotted a building with the letters RESTAURANT painted across the length of its roof reminding us we were hungry.

"Lonche. I'm starving," I said swinging into the rear car park across from a large unmarked white van painted with an enormous orange flower and garish colored fruit on both sides.

"Wow what great artwork decorating van," Susan said reaching for her camera. "Oops. Too late."

For at that moment the driver jumped down, opened up the back and let the van's bedraggled human cargo spill onto the dirt. "One, two, three…fifteen, sixteen, seventeen," we counted seventeen people make their way stiffly towards the roadhouse.

In the washroom, I startled one of the van's cargo with her homespun skirts pulled to her thighs, splashing water between her legs. One foot in the hand basin, fiftyish, the woman froze, her deep brown eyes round with a fear I could only guess at.

"Hola. Buenas Dias," I smiled hoping my greeting assured her I was no threat, and not from ICE.

Quickly finishing her ablutions, she disappeared inside one of the stalls and locked herself in. Remembering my own first difficult days as an immigrant to this country, I pushed a ten-dollar bill under her cubicle door and fled.

By the time Susan and I filled our stomachs; an enchilada each, green for me, red for Susan, and downed a cup of coffee, and were ready to tackle the remaining miles, the flower-painted van with its human cargo was nowhere to be seen.

Too tired, too late, the sky too overcast, the truck's cab too noisy and too cramped to stretch our legs, we gave Three Rivers Petroglyphs and White Sands a miss. All we wanted, was to lie supine in a motel and be still.

"Another time, when the weather's good," we agreed.

"It's special. White Sands," I turned to tell her.

Susan, her head against the window-glass, her mouth open, slept.

The rumbling of the truck for company, the sight of the white dunes rising in the distance sparked a secret memory of the trip with my Galisteo boyfriend to show me his New Mexico the previous spring.

We arrived at White Sands just after dawn as the Park opened, I remembered, and drove way back into the dunes before pulling off the road. Taking off his watch, David told me to leave my shoes in the car. I remember my surprise of the feel of the ice-cold sand underfoot and the squeaking each foot made as we climbed up and over the first rise.

"Should be far enough," David said. "Now your clothes. We'll leave them here." Like him, I stripped, and left them bundled by a cholla cactus, then visually marked the spot in relation to the jagged peaks on either side of the valley.

'We'll meet up in about an hour. O.K? It's best to go alone to experience absolute solitude." David said.

Wearing just hats and sunglasses we set off in opposite directions. Like Lucy, *Hominis Erectus* walking naked in the dawn, I became the only living being in the world. Whitest sand dunes, feathery grasses, deep blue shadows, sapphire sky, distant black mountains. I never felt so euphoric, so free. Pausing my remembering, I turned to tell Susan of my magical experience. Eyes closed, the rhythm of her breathing told me she still slept. The Sands remained my private place. My secret was still my own.

Susan missed the eighteen-mile drive beside the dune dotted plain and the magnificent climb to the pass over the jagged Organ Mountains and down to Las Cruces.

After we'd revived somewhat in the downtown El Paso motel, we set off on foot over the Rio Grande into Ciudad Juarez on a dry run to the tile merchant while it was still light. Not one official glanced up as we motored onto the bridge's no-man's land spanning the sluggish brown strip of water. Peering through the wire fence, not quite believing what we were seeing, there below us, in full view of the bridge, bored as any New Yorkers waiting for a bus, we saw a line of *illegals* waiting to be ferried home after a day's work in the U.S. One person at a time, they clambered onto a wooden platform bound by ropes to a rubber tire. We watched the ferryman pocket their fares, wade into the river and deliver his passenger back home onto Mexican soil. Not one official, neither the American nor Mexican Border Guards took any notice, not even when Susan reached for her camera and snapped a shot. This was back in the eighties when a *wet-back* held an accepted and valued role in the economy, and the infamous wall was not yet a thought.

We discovered my acupuncturist's tile merchant in a back street off the main drag, and found him expecting us. He checked the paper work.

"Come manana, ten hour. Tiles ready." His English worse than my Spanish.

Duty done, we had the rest of the evening to explore. The crowded street leading from the bridge was one long confusing market aimed at Tourists. Too tired to shop and both starving, we flagged a taxi.

Restaurante, bueno, quieto, I directed.

The cabbie chose a restaurant he liked a scruffy place, filled with smoke and the smell of liquor. We didn't argue.

Talk subsided when we, two gringos, unescorted women,

entered and took our seats at a pink Formica-topped table set with cone-shaped bottles of 'Sombrero' hot sauce, both red and green, and cheap paper napkins wedged into a green plastic holder.

"Dos Margaritas. Up con sal, and la carta." I ordered in my best Spanish.

Although we looked bedraggled and unglamorous, a man, entranced by Susan's red hair, bought us each a second margarita before we finished our first. We studiously dipped totopos, chips, into a bowl of fiery salsa and picked the salt from the glass rim.

"Beautiful girl in all world, I want marry." The stranger slipped into the vacant chair at our table, his eyes limpid, adoring.

"Beauty, I want marry, " he repeated. Reaching with his hand, not touching, but wanting desperately to touch, he stroked a halo in the air about her head.

"No es Possible. Tiene very bueno husband, esposo." I told him in Spanglish, she was unavailable and married.

Susan, not understanding, smiled, sipped her drink, but spoke not a word.

"No, Gracias! Ella no le gusta, no like you. Ella casada." I repeated glaring haughtily in my unaccustomed role of chaperone. I pointing to her ring finger.

The more Susan smiled, the more difficult it was to shake off her suitor. We made do with guacamole and salsa for dinner and left. Thankfully, our cabbie knowing his fare was guaranteed, had parked in a vacant lot across the road and was leaning against his cab waiting to drive us back to the border.

Next morning, once again I drove the flatbed across the Rio Grande. In plain sight, as in the previous evening, commuters stood patient in lines along the river bank waiting for the next available rubber-tire ferry to take them to their jobs in the gold-paved U.S.

The merchant loaded the flatbed with three hundred, ten-inch Saltillo Tiles, and wrote out two receipts, one accurate and one wildly fanciful in order to circumvent customs duty.

"Keep this, rosa receipt in right sleeve, this one, amarillo, in left. This Rosa, throw in river after show Mexican Guardia. Then when on bridge, take yellow from sleeve for Americanos. Not say you planning buy long time. Today only see beauty tile and decide buy. Comprende?"

"Left sleeve Americans, right for the Mexicans. Pink for Mexican, Yellow for Americans." Or was it the other way round? A ridiculous scene from an old Bob Hope farce, *On the Way to the Forum* came to mind of the two comedians dressed in togas hopelessly chanting, *The dish without the parsley is the one without the poison. No, the one without the parsley is the one with the poison. No, the one with the parsley is the....*

"Pink for Mexico, yellow for the U.S. No, yellow for…" Like them, Susan and I intoned the instructions.

A nightmare. This was turning into a nightmare. Yellow up my right sleeve, pink up my left. Or was it, pink-right for the Mexicans and yellow-left for the Americans?

Bugger. The sly acupuncturist hadn't said a word about having to lie and pretend we only decided to buy tiles, spur-of-the-moment.

The receipts pricked my skin uncomfortably. Too busy looking at Susan and her flaming tresses, the Mexican Border Guards never glanced at the flatbed. I stared fixedly ahead, my eyes focused on the massive bronze eagle that held a writhing snake in its beak, symbol of Mexico's Quetzalcoatl. Ironic, I thought, both countries sporting eagles.

A pink receipt fluttered over the Rio Grande. Susan tossed it over the guardrail before the flatbed crested the steeply humped bridge, and we started down the five-lane slope towards the waiting U.S. Customs. We giggled. One down. One to go.

"Hello, 'ello. Well now, ladies, what have we here?" The American border guard held our New Mexican Drivers Licenses in his hand, peered at the Saltillo tiles behind the cab carefully scrutinizing the crumpled yellow receipt. He jabbed his pencil towards the loaded bed.

Suspicious, he's suspicious. We're in trouble. We're going to be fined. We'll be held in a cell until we could pay. My terror scrambled unheard.

"Smile, Susan. Smile. Look calm," I whispered, attempting to do the same.

"Well, isn't this the bargain, girls? Paid all of $150, did we? Just happened to be in Juarez with a truck, now did we? Weren't you the lucky ones." He spoke slowly emphasizing each word.

He pulled out a note pad. He bent towards us. His eyes narrowed. Severe, his face almost inside the window. As suddenly as he'd appeared, he stepped away, smiled, tapped his temple, nodding knowingly, and returned his pad and pencil to his left breast pocket. He waved us through.

Grinding into second gear, I crept past America's empty-beaked Winged Guardian of the Bridge, swearing never again. Never. Not ever.

I don't remember the journey back to Santa Fe. We didn't stop. We both wanted the journey over and finished. It was dusk by the time the truck groaned into Galisteo, and Susan's taillights disappeared down the driveway. I flopped beside my boyfriend and slept without stirring.

I made my delivery to the acupuncturist in Santa Fe next morning. Passing the Guadalupe's statue near the Cathedral, I noticed a lone woman offering up a single-stemmed marigold along with her prayers. I swear it was she, that same woman, the one whose foot was in the sink at our *lonche* stop, the one from the orange flowered van. I'm sure of it, because as she caught my eye, she startled as though she'd seen an apparition, then quickly turned back towards the Virgin hands together and bowed her head.

I could tell from my acupuncturist's sheepish smile she was surprised to see me and the truck back safely in one piece and so soon. She refunded my expenses without a murmur, and invited me to her New Year's party, to celebrate her newly tiled floor.

I pocketed my money. I offered her a sculpture for my next trade.

I've come of age. I've passed a milestone, I sang at the close of that first year in '86. Pathetic to be sure, but at the age of 46 I'd eaten my first restaurant meal alone, addressed the waiter directly, and even ordered a lager, two behaviors frowned on for a nice woman back in England. Working my way to graduation, I learned to speak up, say no, ask for what I wanted, drank beer from a jam jar, and in a smoky dance bar even asked a cowboy for a dance. I'm I. I'm me. I schooled myself to no longer referring to myself as one. Whoa. Progress. I wondered at the brazen American I had become. I took myself out to lunch to celebrate.

LUNCH AT CHOWS

"The moon is hollow." The man at the restaurant table next to mine leaned towards his lunch companion. "But you know that, of course." The man's red-striped tie swept across his plate.

"Well," his companion nodded, "You never see the other side of the moon, now do you? "They…" he emphasized they, "never show you its far side do they? Never."

I didn't quite follow his logic. Selecting a grain of rice and clamping it between my chopsticks, I concentrated on lifting it to my mouth so my neighbors wouldn't guess I was hanging on their every word,

My two lunch friends, Ellen and Joan, continued chatting assuming I was just too busy eating to join in. I tapped Ellen's arm—interrupting her account of some altercation her dogs had with….

"Crazy." I mouthed turning to my girlfriends. I crossed my eyes and lolled my tongue to one side of my open mouth.

"What?" Ellen yelled loudly enough for the two men to hear.

Joan's eyebrows arched.

"I thought you were clever at guessing games," I sniggered. "Clever enough to get it—my meaning." I jabbed my finger surreptitiously at the neighboring table. "The moon is hollow, don't you know."

"Are you nuts?" She stared puzzled.

Head averted from the two men, I crossed my eyes again.

"Them," I whispered in explanation. "They say…they know… the moon is hollow."

"Ridiculous." Ellen hissed. "Everybody and his dog know the moon is filled with dog's bones.

The devil gets into me sometimes. It's not intentional. Fearfully embarrassing when I realize how badly I've behaved. Usually, it happens when I find myself doing something I really don't want to do. Like being obligated to admire someone's new carpet, for goodness sake. Should have refused of course, but this happened back on a trip to England before I learned the magic power of the two letter word N-O.

CATS LOVE CHIMNEYS

"Love you to come over. See it in situ. Round teatime then?"

Some casual friends, not good friends, asked me over to admire their carpet of their London house over the road from mine. "…professionally laid," they added proudly.

I cannot imagine why I agreed, or what possessed me to say what I said. I was standing on the pure wool sea in their living room, when their white cat stalked towards me, tail straight, and rubbed against my leg.

"Cats love chimneys," I pronounced, remembering my father pointing our own puss, Pootsie, towards the fireplace in our country home when I was a child, and how she'd disappeared. Forever, I thought, the first time I saw her leap claws out as she did when she climbed the Dutch Elm by the driveway to stare back at us from between the leaves like Alice's Cheshire Cat and refusing to come down. But she'd always re-appeared from her adventure skyward up the flue, excited, wild-eyed with what she'd seen or imagined she had seen. Chimney climbing became her daily ritual when the fire was not alight.

Rather than admire my friends' carpet a moment longer, I'd already cooed, "Lovely. How nice," I repeated to my hosts, "Cats love chimneys. Really. They really do. Here, I'll show you." And I scooped their city puss into my arms and pointed her up the chimney as I'd seen my father point Pootsie, although I had never actually done it myself, and without knowing if there was some special call she and my father shared to bring her safely back.

Gone. Disappeared. My hosts' pampered city cat scampered

up their chimney flue. The three of us watched transfixed, Beryl, her poet-actor husband, Peter, and me, as soot flakes floated into the grate. Faint scratching told us she was alive.

"Diddie, Diddie," they pleaded. "Here… Puss, Puss," but I was silent for white cats are deaf, I'd heard, and I wasn't about to remind them. I was thinking of the Fire Brigade and wondering if this counted as an emergency, and if the roof and wall would have to be demolished to hoick stuck Diddie out.

"What about a flashlight?" I suggested.

While Beryl ran to fetch one, Peter fell to his hands and knees twisting his neck to see if he could sight her, when, plop, Diddie thudded into the empty grate, pure white no longer.

Treading black pads across the white expanse, she evaded Peter's outstretched hands and streaked towards the door. Pausing in the doorway, Diddie surveyed us for an instant, her tail erect, her eyes as wild as Pootsie's had always been when she returned from the magic of the black tunnel and glimpsed her secret world.

"Thank God. She's safe. Oh. Diddie, Diddie," Beryl cried throwing daggers in my direction, her eyes squeezed narrow to ensure they struck their target.

"See," I replied, before I fled never to be invited to their house again, "Cats do love chimneys."

The Land of the Free. So much talk of Past Lives, Gurus, Aura Balancing, Chakras, Self-help, Alien Abductions, Roswell and such, was too much, too strange to take in. Bombarded by strange and new ideas, my heads spun. It took a little time for me to weed out what didn't interest me and discover what helped me grow.

I attached myself to a group who followed a Hindu Philosophy that suited, and made me happy. One teacher, one path, I loved their chanting, learned the power of meditation and how to quiet my mind. I visited an Ashram for the first time. Delved deep inside myself through many of their courses. India was the logical next step. Oh yes, I yearned to return to the land of my birth and spend time in Siddha Yoga's ashram outside Mumbai.

ONLY IN INDIA

Things happen in India that don't quite happen elsewhere in the world, I discovered.

Seva, my daily duties chopping vegetables, over for a few hours, dreaming along the winding country lane outside the Ashram towards the small village of Ganeshpuri where hot springs bubbled from the river, and I could soak in the bathhouse there for less than a dollar, I came across a flock of chickens pecking at a cowpat splodged in the middle of the road. Not a soul in sight, I stopped to watch them. Peck. Peck. Peck. Happy, happy, chickens at one with their chicken world.

Choook-chook-choooook, I chooked as I used to as a child.

Choook-chook-choooook they answered.

Choook-chook-choooook, I answered back.

For a couple of seconds, I stood among them exchanging chooks.

All of a sudden, a saddhu, a man I swear wasn't there before, materialized right in front of me and the birds looking as holy men are supposed to look, orange robed, beaded, and with flowing beard and hair.

"Yes, God's brethren speak to us in many tongues," he remarked with a smile staring deep into my eyes.

Feeling extremely foolish, I nodded, scurrying sideways passed him. When I turned back, he'd vanished, poof.

Though, he's long disappeared, his words stay with me to this day. A frog, a horse, a guinea hen, I listen to every creature's song.

A different day, and the only Westerner visiting the temple shrine, I watched a group of young women laughingly attempt to stick coins on the granite wall of the shrine.

Lots of luck I thought. Well, coins don't stick to smooth stone without glue, though I did see a fair number decorating the wall.

"Come, have a go," they called me. "It's very auspicious, if one sticks."

I chose an anna from my purse, stepped forward and pressed the tiny coin hard against the wall's surface. It stuck.

I don't know who was more startled, them, or me. They eyed me oddly, then bending, touched my feet as if I had special powers.

I'd dropped everything the second I saw the documentary showing the ashram's annual eye camp and the doctors at work. Twelve hundred cataracts took six surgeons from abroad just ten minutes to remove each sightless veil. Led by a relative, many patients had walked for days to reach the camp. Unlike same-day surgery of Western countries, they and their bandages stayed on five days as a safeguard from infection, for many patients living without adequate sanitation.

The wonder on the faces of those who could see again. Those, who perhaps for years had never seen the limpid color of their grandchild's and spouse's eyes, and their son's bride. As the eye bandages lifted, the astonishment and joy of the people seeing again made everyone present break down in tears.

I imagined myself white-over-alled, floating between beds and lifting water to grateful, thirsty lips. But rightly of course, reality replaced my prideful dreams.

Only properly qualified staff were assigned to tend the shifting 200 patient population of the tented eye camp.

In order for the helpers to eat, cooks cooked, sweepers swept, water carriers, nurse aids did their specific jobs. And me? I chopped. My Seva, was chopper. And how we choppers chopped. Aproned, hands washed, each day, twice a day sometimes, we sat on our stools before stainless steel tables waiting to be handed our knives. First came the demonstration. Exactly this size, this thickness, our supervisor menaced holding up the sample veg. slice she wanted copied.

Take the day off, I was rewarded after a week. So, with a seva-buddy, we crossed the road to the tailor opposite the ashram's main gates. Fluttering his hands, the tailor raised his eyes to heaven, repeating, Maha Shakti. Maha Shakti. Great energy. Great Must see. And he motioned towards a small Ashram down a side road, and the name of a holy Master we couldn't catch.

Why not? We thought, and set off along the country lane he indicated in our newly tailored clothes. Passing a row of neat mud-built huts, fascinated to see women sweeping their hard dirt yards clean of dust. We'd gone about a mile, when the unusual sound of a pneumatic drill coming from the ashram grounds fractured the peace.

We climbed the concrete steps to the entrance, removed our sandals, and entered a long, narrow hall. Odd we whispered indicating a group of loudly weeping women at the far end of the hall. We lowered ourselves to the floor seating ourselves opposite the unknown Master's photo to check the protocol as people disappeared and reappeared through a distant doorway. Clearly, we should too and followed a woman through the door. There at the bottom of a short flight of steps sat the Master we'd come to see. Perfectly posed, unmoving, sitting crossed legged on a string charpoy sat the Master in full lotus. Eyes closed, smiling, naked but for a loincloth, flower garlands and a string of 52 wooden Rudraksha beads about his neck, he sat in a meditation so deep, so serenely peaceful, I fell respectfully to my knees. Whoa, I thought gazing at his form, I've heard about yogis like this.

And as I knelt, I realized pools of puddled water on the floor melting from huge ice blocks.

I raised my head and gazed upon the Holy man. His chest was still. No breath flowed.

"Katrina," I mouthed to my friend. "He's dead." My too loud whisper resounded. Now I understood.

Maha Shakti. The Master had been dead for thirty-six hours. The drilling we heard was for his tomb. The deep pit, where bathed in salt crystals he would sit in lotus posture for eternity. We bowed low and left.

Returning later that afternoon, we found the Master crowned and seated upright on a bullock cart almost buried beneath garlands of orange and lotus flowers for the procession to the Ganeshpuri Temple, two miles away. Mournful trumpets, the funereal beat of drums, clashing finger cymbals and heady incense preceded the cortege. An attendant stood behind the corpse to prevent the Master keeling sideways or his jaw from dropping.

The Temple doors were flung wide to reveal the black basalt statue of the Master's Master, the Guru's Guru. As the cart circled and stopped allowing them to face each other for a final moment together on this earthly plane, three tears trickled from the Master's sightless eyes to course down his lifeless cheeks. I swear it. I saw his tears.

Hopefully a little wiser, a little more aware, a little more at peace, I returned to New Mexico from India. Yes, life was perfect, I sighed.

CHAIN REACTION

Opposing directions connected. Yet not. Horizontal. Down. Sideways. Across. Zig-zag. Zig-zags. Lines fill an empty page. . If I'd just not been… done… and I had never… then would…? My mind races. Say thank-you. Thank-you. I shut my eyes. Will myself to go on.

I couldn't have guessed my being injured in a road accident would lead to a chain of incidents that as it turned out saved my own life. When I think of each connection, how one little action led to another, another and then another, I hold my breath struck by the magnitude of the unseen super power I know kept me alive.

Zig. The beginning… I'm desperate to go to India. Land of my birth. It will be the first time since I turned seven and sailed Home to a country I'd never known.

Zag…August. I'm meditating in the Ashram temple, New York. When can I go to India I pray. Not till you have paid off all your debts. The message loud and clear startles me. Okay. Okay. Got it, I reply. Bow. Get to my feet. Stumble outside. $35,000 in debt. How will I ever find such a sum?

Oh Goddess of wealth, please favor me, Back in New Mexico I pray to her every day. In my studio, I focus on my work. Ship off ten metal sculptures to Toronto, Canada for my first and only one-person show. Somehow escape export, import, and Custom's tax.

Zig. October. Guest of honor, I attend the show. All but two small works sell. Unheard of in my artist's world. I count the cash. A miracle. Thank you, I whisper pressing my Albuquerque-Mumbai ticket to my chest.

Zag. February. I loan my house to a couple of meditation friends for the six weeks I'll be gone.

We'll drive you. Go on. You sit in the front seat, they both insist. It's six am. Husband, Rob driving, Rebecca, his wife, in the back, we set off for the airport. I've allowed four extra hours, time enough to share a leisurely breakfast with a girlfriend. Rush hour by the time we reach

Bernalillo. Fifteen miles to go. LOOK OUT. A ladder fallen from the truck ahead of us blocks the road. Rob, my friend, swerves to miss it. Pulls the wheel left too hard steering the car into the fast lane. Fearing we'll be hit, he over corrects. Next thing the car's sailing through the air. Airborne. Drops fifteen feet. This can't be happening, screams my mind. I'm flying to India today. Mud clots striking the windscreen, obliterate my vision. Further thought. Thump. Thump. Thump. Three times we roll. Three times the car roof strikes the dirt. Then silence. I'm hanging upside down. Om Namah Shiva, our shared mantra shimmers in the quiet. Everyone OK? Rebecca, Rob and I each whisper. They unbuckle, drop onto the roof and crawl outside. The head of a young stranger peers at me through the window. Reaches in. Unbuckles my strap. I drop onto glass chips from where he pulls me out. My passport. My passport's inside, I point. I'll get it. No worries, the young stranger soothes, and does.

Fire trucks, cops, an ambulance swarm the scene. Insist they check for broken limbs, concussion. Adrenalin rush, I'm speedy. I've a flight to catch. I'm going to India, I struggle past.

You're not going anywhere, ma'am. The policeman holds me back. If you're going anywhere, you're going to hospital.

It took a lot of argumenting and lies to convince both emergency services and police to allow on my way. Not to the ER.

Rob and Rebecca. Their car totaled, I never saw them after that till I returned. The stranger and his wife delivered me and my bags to the airport.

Buckled into my plane-seat and up in the air, I sobbed. Don't worry, I explained to my seat neighbor. I'm just in shock. Three bumps on my skull swelled. Egg-sized. Bled a little. Eight hours. Longer. The flight slipped me into the following day.

Mumbai. The Ashram had no Physio therapist I could see. There's a woman in the village who does bodywork, they told me. And so I found Rosie. She would work on my bruised body for five dollars a session. Every day we met. Every day we laughed and liked the little more we learned about the other. A prostitute, the ignorant labeled her. A single woman living alone, touching naked bodies? Well. We hugged before I left and promised to remember our time together.

Six weeks later, back home, Christmas came and a New Year began.

February a year later. Odile, a French nurse friend, was soon to leave for the Ashram. In a shopping bag, I parceled a woolen cardigan, warm rug, hand mirror and other gifts. These, for Rosie, I pleaded. Give them to her with my love. Two months later, Odile returned and handed me a small bundle of newspaper. Inside, a photograph of our shared Spiritual teacher and a tiny silver ghee wick holder to light on my puja, and a brown knitted cap to keep cold night airs from my head during pre-dawn meditation. With love and blessings, for your protection, Rosie. A scrap of paper read.

Snow retreated. The earth greened.

Yet more zig-zags to negotiate lie ahead. Invisibly linked, though I'm still not wise to their connections. It's not the end.

April. I planned a drive to Salt Lake City. My eldest son was to present a talk at the Cued Speech conference. I rose before dawn, locked the front door and set the alarm. I started the car. Then, switched off the engine. I need to take the photo Rosie gave me. The thought persistent, I unstrapped myself from my safety belt. Exiting the car I retraced my steps, unlocking, relocking the door behind me. Lost a few minutes at most. Driving West, beyond Jemez Pueblo, the sun rose from behind flooding the New Mexican desert ahead. Pink. Purple-red. The road climbed steeply through a maze of towering rocks. America the beautiful, Oh beautiful, I sang, dazed to all around me. Rounding a bend, I gasped. Slammed my brakes. A massive Semi stopped, slued across my path. Pieces of what used to be a car littering the highway. A man's body immobile. One leg angled, clearly broken. Noises gurgled bubbling from his throat. Rushing to him, I placed a blanket beneath his head, held his hand, placed his driver's-license on his chest and called his name. Seeing a crucifix about his neck, I put one hand over his heart. Rest it gently. The Lord's my shepherd, I'll not want, He makes me down to lie... I sang to him aloud ...in pastures green he leadeth me the... My voice echoed from the surrounding cliffs. Drowned as rescue helicopter landed between the Semi, my car and where he lay. Doctors, nurses feverish inside a triage tent. Half an hour, an hour, I couldn't guess. I sat hunkered shivering in my car. Stable enough at last, the helicopter whisked the man's broken body to the sky.

A State Trooper approached. Bent his beanpole form to peer at me inside. His hands lightly rested on my open window. Pale face. He melted, transparent, ethereal. Was he real? Blue eyes, piercing, bored my soul. Disassembled he became an angel transported to deliver me God's message.

I want to thank you ma'am. Not everyone would have stopped. Several minutes, maybe seconds, we held each other's gaze.

A stranger helped me once, I stuttered.

And as he waved me on my way, fat teardrops, unstoppable rolling from my eyes, I sobbed thanked Rosie aloud for saving my life. But for my car wreck all those months back, … if I'd not sought out Rosie…

But for those extra seconds I took to go back indoors for the photo she gave me… I knew for certain it would have been me lying on the road. Me, the Semi hit.

Back in the groove, my mother's companion, for a little separate time from her, I often took myself down to the plaza in Santa Fe. Not so dissimilar from England's villages set around what we English call a Common, was my first thought thinking of the bare-kneed medieval Morris Dancers cavorting there on a summer's day back home. Wrong, the mix of cultures, the swirl of color, the chile smell, the clack of heeled boots there in the Plaza, I hardly knew which way to turn. Settled on a shady bench, though I tried to hide it, I couldn't help but stare. Men in cowboy hats, men decked out in jewelry and men with long flowing hair and cruising low-riders driving cars I'd only seen in movies. So much to soak in.

After grey old England, I'd be blind not to be bowled over by the beauty, color, the sights and sounds of Santa Fe.

Back in a corner of my bedroom, beginning from the upper right, I selected and replaced each crayon in its new box. One by one I scribbled patches of every subtle color gradation to form my color wheel. I propped my handiwork against a chair, stepped back and stared. Each tone, each shade contributed to the whole. Complete, balanced, I taped it to the wall.

Painters don't leave a canvas devoid of color, nor I my sculptures. My cut-out figures would be nothing without their brilliant powder-coated colors.

BETTER RED THAN BLUE

"Could we survive?" The fair-haired youth, and the girl asked, "If, stripped of clothing, we walked deep into White Sands? Could we survive one full night and day prey to the sun's relentless probe, the desert's penetrating cold? Would our brains sizzle maddening us to gobble sand?"

Their quest was not that they should depart this Earth, rather that their suffering might induce visions of things not normally seen; to better understand their place on Earth; know which roads to tread; perhaps bring forth a message of some betterment to offer man.

"We'll carry but a single pebble," they both agreed.

Between fronds of tamarisk in the creek bed below their yurt, each picked a pebble that sang their song. Saliva-inducing to moisten swollen tongues. Sweat saltlick. A pebble they could not live without.

Before the park closed a friend dropped them far inside the dunes. A marker West. A marker East, they chose their landmarks aligned between two mountain peaks, strung a string of twine on a cholla-cactus skeleton, removed their clothes.

"Race You."

He chasing. She evading. Playful. Naked. They sprinted toward the first horizon imprinting heel-hollows, the digits of their toes in the sand. Avoiding jagged yucca-spurs and blades of razorgrass, they followed lines etched by lizard tails, and toe-prints tracked by kangaroo mice; traced their fingers along a rattler's wavy trail. Bending, the boy and girl drew images of their own.

No longer suspended, the sun's orb spilled red and purple-blues into shadowed valleys. Horizons pleating the desert, they sat close. Watched the moon sink. Vanish behind the horizon.

Prostrate in a hollow, the youth pressed his length to hers drawing day's warmth from sand scuffed tight against their skin, the girl laid her head against the crooked arm of the boy sighing, watching, as Venus, the Pleiades, then other stars, and yet others they could not name blinked their greeting to the night. Palms flat on one-another's bellies, they slept.

Awaking, they stretched, shook the sprinkling of silver sand from their eyelids, hair and from their browned skin. Soft hairs on the girl's tanned thighs, her arms and belly lifted seeking heat. She shivered. The youth's erection saluted the dawn. *Not today*, they both laughed. Obedient, his member bowed its head.

The sand cold, the air delightful, fresh. The youth tapped his wrist, mimed two hours, pointing out a dune distanced in a violet valley. With his fore and middle finger he gestured first his eyes then back to where they stood. The girl nodded. Understood.

Blowing him a kiss, she turned and made for her experience of what it was to be alone in a desolate land.

He became invisible to her, and she to him.

Hands and knees. Climbing. Her breath came short. Summiting, she stood, offered up her pebble, slowly circled, once, twice, three times. She drew a sundial with her heel, marked the sun. Then facing North, erased both mountain ranges from her view. Only sand and sky remained. To see nothing was her goal.

Draped flat, breasts heavenward, pelvis wriggled down, her young body melded with the ridgeline. Open-eyed, unblinking, infinity faded, the girl's world swam cerulean blue. Drowsy, her lids fluttered. Closed, her world veined red velvet. Opened, she saw the vastness above was not empty. Transparent light beads swirling, spinning, traced spirals like those depicted in Hokusai's etchings and Oriental silk-embroidered hangings that they saw then what she was seeing, she knew those spirals were real. Space was full. Sky held no emptiness. She sat bolt upright, her mouth open. "I know those patterns." The girl's whisperings rude in the silence. "others seen them too!"

She folded her legs. Sat some more. Absorbed.

Her own footprints led her back to where she'd left him standing. A mirage, arms wide, a Christ-beacon, he received her. Motionless, they faced one another, the pounding of their two hearts the only sound. They smiled.

The youth bent, his tongue lapping, licked the sweat-crease below the girl's breasts. Bending, she licked his neck-hollow, belly, his armpits. Savored brief relief.

Walking, they came upon Buzzard feathers. Remnants of a kill. He plucked and placed three wing feathers in her hair. A fringe for her eyes. She poked three plumes into his curls. The rest they carried to two burrows scooped earlier from a steep slope. Hunkered in the shade pool below the surface, they wove two feather caps, padded them with buzzard-down. Insulated their brains.

Stilled beneath the arcing sun, fixated on imagined desert pools, heard water splash, and turned their faces to drink the cool. Delirious. Sometimes panicked, they struggled to keep from running, screaming. Wild for death.

Breath in. Breath Out. Eyes shut. Red. Eyes open. Blue. Day crept. The boy, the girl transcended their agony.

"I am a stupid fool. I am a stupid fool." The youth mouthed three thousand lines.

"Is red better than blue? Is blue better than red?" Her question, like the pebble in her mouth, rolled inside her head.

I missed my family, home, friends and the countryside. I wanted to sit under real trees, oaks large enough for kings to hide in, and gaze on hills and fields of real green. I missed the Pubs, I missed all of England's countryside with its riotous hedgerows spilling dog rose and campion. I found a deal, bought a ticket, and hopping across the pond squeezed hold of my boys. I'm home, yes, home, I shouted pushing open my front door. We partied weekends and reunited with family and friends.

Spur of the moment, deciding to look up Loveday, a friend I hadn't seen since I lived in Bahrain ten years before, I knocked on her door.

DOWNFALL

My…could fifteen years have sped by since last we'd met, fifteen years since we both lived in Bahrain. She, the virgin wife of an English Arabist lawyer and me, a neglected Royal Naval officer's wife. Two women desperate to break free from the rigid lives in which we'd found ourselves. Both artists, finding someone with interests other than the weather and non-sensical chit-chat was beyond miraculous.

Ready? She'd ask as I settled side saddle onto the back of her Vesper clutching my painting stool, and off we'd ride.

We painted together several times a week, au plein air, still-lives of her long-beaked copper, coffee pot resting beside bright persimmons and orange fruit. Always somewhere safe-ish for two unescorted women to be alone in public, we sketched a Sheik's Palace, a minaret, the Portuguese ruins, a walled desert village, a palm-treed oasis, and from the deck of my husband's ship, a fleet of Dhows bobbing the diamond studded deep blue sea. As it was, a watching crowd soon jostled around us noting our every move often forcing us to pack up and ride her scooter home. Overlooking neighbors' courtyards from our rooftops, we immortalized ordinary family lives in oil paint on canvas boards: unveiled women, children, and their flock of scrawny chickens.

So lively back then, Loveday introduced me to the Bahraini culture, and through her I met her veiled Bahraini women friends and picked up a smattering of Arabic.

Persian copper vessels, nomadic saddlebags and silk carpets decorated every corner of her house. She helped me choose a silver bangle in Manama's eerily silent Suq where no sound could be heard but the light pad of feet, a swish of satin from womens' *abbas* as their hooded forms passed me by.

One outing into empty sand-duned desert, I'll never forget— the good-bye party my husband's fellow officers held for us in a far oasis beneath a clutch of date palms where blue shade pooled in the still burning setting sun. Sipping wine, sprawled on Persian rugs while mint-laced rice and mutton simmered, the charcoal's flare, the sinking orange orb, the myriad winking pinpricks in a Prussian blue/black sky, and the glory of the emptiness is a scene imprinted forever in my mind.

Back in England, wanting to reminisce, I looked up my friend.

A wispy grey-haired woman held open the door.

"Lordy, Loveday. Whatever has happened to you?" I blurted recoiling slightly from the bony fingers extended towards me from the folds of the woman's patched tweed skirt. Her skin dull, pale and ethereal as if she no longer lived on earth. Everything about her faded…her hair, powdery skin. The very bones of her slumped.

"I know," she said with a wry half-smile, "It's why I never called you before…"

Stacked three-foot high two sides of the pokey bed-sit, the piles of dusty books with their red, yellow and rainbow slipcovers, glared at odds with the peeling paper on the walls. Shoeboxes, a suitcase poked from beneath her single bed. I smelled decay.

Remembering the confident woman she'd been, and the adventures we'd once shared. I looked around for some object— any vestige of her past. Surely, she'd kept something, just one reminder of her Bahrain days. But nothing. Not even a copper bowl.

Gone her rugs, her Persian furnishings, the exotic harem decor of her Bahrain home. Gone her youth, the straw halo of her hair.

Loveday motioned me to her only armchair. Pulled up an oak spindle-back for herself and settled opposite me.

"It's good to see you again," I smiled, hoping she wouldn't hear the hollow knock of my lie. I couldn't remind her. Pain her.

"You too," she answered handing me a crumpled newspaper cutting.

"Here, read this while I make the tea."

"What...?" I faltered. Starred, dated I scanned the headline she'd circled.

"Yes," she said. "It's all true. I keep the clipping to prove I'm not making it all up."

"A lot has happened in the fifteen years since we both left Bahrain," Loveday's voice dropped to barely a whisper. I leaned forward to catch her words.

The hiss of gas heating the water-kettle filled the hovering silence. Then like the Ancient Mariner, she held me hostage with the telling of her tale....

"You remember I had my marriage to Brian annulled?" Loveday hesitated. "After so many years, oh Lord was I desperate to lose my virginity..."

I back-flipped fifteen years to an image of her standing before her easel focused studiously on working a blob of paint while she blurted out her confession.

Her driver had dropped us off in the shaded grove where a fresh water pool flowed to the row of scrubbing stones where women gathered to launder their garments. Arms bare, their black veils pushed back, they laughed together as if they understood the enormity of what Loveday was telling me—*A virgin, still, after seven years?* Yes, the idea was laughable. And I remember Loveday had gone on to tell me of her wedding night spent sitting in Gatwick airport's waiting lounge with their bags because, Brian insisted as he had a paranoid fear of missing flights. *Weird*, she'd thought uneasily after he insisted that they spend their second night in Paris' Orly's airport lounge, the third in Rome's airport, and the next in Istanbul's. Every stopover. *Finally*, she'd thought when they arrived on the tiny island of Bahrain. *Now I'll lose my virginity.* But no, despite anger, flirting, tears, her seductive dance of the seven veils, nothing could entice her husband to make love to her.

"Oh, the shame. Who could I confide in with only ten of us Brits living there. And all of them friends of Brian's?"

I recall the anger in my friend's words, the way she spat them out, the furrows deepening across her forehead. I kept silent.

"…and by the time I did return on home leave two years later, I just couldn't face the shame of it," she continued. "I couldn't possibly TELL. Not anyone. After two years of marriage? And still no consummation? How could I possibly confess and shame myself and Brian?"

I nodded, recalling, but not mentioning, the scandal of her houseboy's attempted rape, the whispered story of his jumping on her naked form spread-eagled on her bed…the hint of the door left invitingly ajar…the punishing disgrace that followed.

"But this is what you don't know…what happened after I finally had our marriage annulled.

Once the Divorce Courts set me free from Brian I went on the hunt. Grabbed the first man I happened on, in my case a brawny handyman at the London Secretarial College where I taught. God the Sex. Hot. Hot. Couldn't get enough." Loveday bit her lip her eyes shining with triumph.

"Jack was his name," she added staring at me as if suddenly remembering my presence.

"Go on," I nodded unable to picture the sex siren my friend

described.

"Within a week, he, Handyman-Jack as I called my lover, moved into my flat. On the ground floor, the rooms double French doors opened onto the most glorious rose garden and lush green lawn I'd ever seen…actually they were the reason for renting the place. What a contrast to the pathetic patch of desert I tried to nurture all those years in Bahrain."

Though the kettle had boiled, instead of pouring the water into the teapot, Loveday switched off the gas with all thoughts of tea forgotten, plumped down onto the wooden chair and pulled it to face me, knees almost touching.

"Living in sin, Charles, my brother, called it when I told him I'd taken a lover.

'Be careful, Sis,' was all he said." Loveday glanced sideways at me and sighed.

"Jack had been living with me about six weeks when I first noticed. Small items at first went missing; my silver dollar ash-tray, an antique incense burner. Jack turned vague when I asked if he'd seen them. And uneasy as I was, foolishly let the matter drop.

Returning home from work one afternoon a few weeks later, exhausted, I kicked off my shoes and flopped out on the sofa. Opposite me an empty space glared from the wall where my Kashmiri Prayer rug hung.

'What have you done with my rug?' I accused, jumping up and screeching like a banshee.

Jack flushed and made to strike me, then suddenly crumpled.

'Why, Jack? Why? If its money you wanted, you only needed to ask.' Can't believe my stupidity, but I reached out my hands to him instead of throwing the rotten bugger out onto the street.

'I couldn't face begging from you again, so I hocked it. Got a hundred pounds. Forgive me?' Emboldened by my weakness he wheedled, his head against my chest. Worth ten times more, no point to say anything, I let the matter drop.

Over the following weeks, other valuables disappeared one by one. My purse emptied. I should have called the police, of course… But I still loved the rotten bastard. Craved his sex. Then over night he changed. Took to the bottle. Turned jealous. Mean. Brooded about the people I met at work, and even what we'd spoken about. It was the whiskey that did it.

'This? Is this what you went looking for? Bitch,' he'd yell dragging me bed-ward by my hair."

Loveday's voice cracked. "Jack's love-making became more like rape. I suppose I should have, could have spoken up sooner and insisted Jack explain. A part of me niggled I should confront him but I couldn't risk the thought of his leaving. You see, passion still clouded my senses."

Like a priest in a confessional, I was trapped. With no possible escape, on and on, my friend's words battered my ears.

"One day, exhausted, just back from a hot day's teaching, my only thought was of my garden, my bare toes wriggling in its cool green grass, and the restorative fragrance of my roses when I pushed open the double doors." Her face crumpled. "I nearly fainted," she continued. "Not a rosebush, not a chrysanthemum, not a blade of grass, every bush charred ghosts, blacked remnants of my beloved garden, stretched before me. The scorched trunk of the chestnut tree, the only living thing. 'Whaah…ah ah aaah.' Unable to stop, my screams frightened even me, brought my neighbors to their windows. Then I smelt it. Gasoline. I smelt what lay ahead. I knew I must escape. Carefully. Without alerting him, my Handyman-Jack, of my fear, I tried to carry on as normal for the next few days, but we made sure we never met and if we did, never speak. If he was home, I stayed out. The weekend loomed. We'd talk then.

Saturday, half way through my toast and marmalade, the sun-room door pushed open. Jack rumpled from bed and bowed down by guilt, slunk into the room and shuffled to the coffee pot. His hand shook. A stranger's eyes gazed at me across the table avoiding mine. 'Mornin.' He mumbled.

Studiously opening mail, I pushed a letter towards him. 'Eviction notice…the garden…'

Silence. Jack's head dropped.

'I'll be staying with my brother, Charles.' I announced, my voice, ice, firm. 'He'll be round for me in an hour.'

'Don't leave…' Jack's sniveling tears, snot bubbles. Disgusting.

'I'll get treatment. Swear! God's truth, I will. Dry-out. One more chance, Pl-e-a-s-e…'

The doorbell rang. 'It's Charles.' I said, rising.

Packed, I slammed the door and was gone. Two weeks passed. No sign of Jack. My brother's flat, a haven. Calm. Me, grateful his told-you-so remained unsaid. Not a word of blame. Free. I was free. I began to breathe again.

Then…the phone rang.

'Jack here, Loveday, my love. I'm out. Discharged from rehab. I'll drive round and pick you up. I need to see you. Let's go somewhere and talk. Please.'

I owe him that much, I stupidly convinced myself. A mistake, I knew, the minute I got into the car beside him."

Thankfully, Loveday paused. She briefly closed her eyes as she relived her nightmare. Hooked, her story had me hungry for more.

"You didn't? You didn't get into his car?" I exclaimed.

Loveday nodded, bit her lip before continuing. As if in a hurry to get the story out and done with, her words gathered speed.

"I could tell Jack was on edge. Nervous. He ground the gears. Once skimmed the curb. I remember clutching my safety belt.

'Where are you taking me? Isn't this the motorway? We agreed, coffee round the corner... half an hour... remember?' But Jack didn't answer. His face set. He gripped the wheel. Intent. I turned looking back, uneasy. Something smelled funny. On the backseat, a row of four red five-gallon containers. An image of my charred rose garden flashed. Gasoline. God! Oh! God! He's planning to burn me. My head spun. I mustn't let him guess I know what he's up to.' So, suddenly icy calm, faking a moan, I clasped my mouth pretending a heave. 'Jack! Jack! I'm going to throw-up... Pull over quick... there in that lay-by.'

Oh, thank God. My ruse worked. Jack slammed the brakes slewing crazily off the highway. Even as his car was moving, I opened the door, jumped out onto the road, running into the on-coming traffic waving my arms and hollering, 'Help! Help! He plans to kill me.'

A car swerved, screeched to a stop."

Remembering, Loveday's eyes opened wide. Unseeing. Caught up in the horror, my hands flew to my cheeks in aghast as Loveday resumed.

"They, my stranger-saviors sped me away. 'No not to the police,' I persuaded. 'Take me to my brother's...I beg you.' He wasn't home of course.

'Lock the door. I'll be right there,' my brother commanded over the phone.

Eternity. At last, I heard his, Charles's, key. He held me close. Half stumbling, questions, answers, a cup of sweet tea, my breathing slowed and color crept into my cheeks. Calm. It's okay, Sis. You're safe now.

'Mr. Jack's missing. On the run.' The hospital informed when my brother called.

'What to do? He's coming to get me.' I've never been so pan-icked. Charles double-checked the door was locked then dialed

999. 'Police?' Charles looked severe. 'We're to keep away from the windows and doors and wait here, they said.'

Pouring each of us a double whiskey, my brother and I eked out the wait chatting childhood do you remember whens…? Till the scream of fire engines, police cars and ambulance outside didn't pass. Sounded close. Continued too long. Cracking open the curtains, spotlit, the High Street three floors below glared day-bright. Fire engines' colored lights spun red on a crowd of upturned faces. Charles and I backed away and ran, but just as we reached for the front door, a megaphone boomed, 'Keep back! Keep back! Stay back from your door.' Then came the crackle of Walkie-talkies, and sounds we couldn't place. Twenty minutes. Maybe an hour. Not speaking, confused, straining to make sense of what was happening outside, we sat. When, CRACK. A steel blade protruded through the front door. Crack. Crack. Wood splintered. An axe struck. Again. Again. 'Police. Police. Stand back stand back. We're coming in.' I remember I screamed as the door fell inward, its pretty blue paint blistered, smoking. Uniformed Bobbies crowded the hall. An ambulance in the street wailed. Faded. A policeman gently put his hand on my shoulder. 'Madam, you need to sit down,' he said. 'I am sorry to inform you there's been an accident…' The Sergeant looked grim. 'We'll need you to identify the remains …unidentified male … petrol … torched himself against your front door…These? All that was left," he said, handing me a pair of blackened steel-rimmed spectacles, their lenses smoked, splintered into stars. 'Belong to anyone you know?' That did it. I couldn't help myself. Hysterical, shocked, I laughed. I couldn't stop. The more I heard my own laughter, the harder I laughed. Half sobbing, I laughed and laughed. They're Jack's. I bought those for him a month ago,' I finally managed to gasp."

Loveday fell silent.

"Difficult to believe, isn't it?" Loveday addressed me. Now you see why I keep the newspaper cutting."

Loveday leaned over and retrieved the scrap of newsprint from the carpet where it had fallen from my lap and handed it to me again.

"JILTED. MAN IMMOLATES HIMSELF ON LOVER'S DOORSTEP."

"Now you understand how I've come to this," she forced a smile, indicating her squalid flat with a wry wave. Salt tears blurred the headlines. I had nothing to say. That was the last time we met.

A month later, under OBITUARIES, the deaths column, I read her name in the Daily Telegraph. A week later I attended her funeral. Wept for my friend at her graveside.

I pulled from my wrist an intricately worked Persian silver bracelet the treasured birthday gift she'd given me all those years before in Bahrain I dropped it on her coffin, and whispered,

"Goodbye Loveday, dear friend. One of your treasures for you to take with you…a precious memento of the good times you spent on earth."

Back in New Mexico for my third winter, stripped of color, the trees trembled stark and naked, and I, no longer able to work outdoors, retreated behind four walls. With the T-shirt brigade gone, and school in session, collectors returned to Santa Fe and galleries hummed with art lovers.

"Good news," our sales director called, "a customer bought two of your seven-feet high works and wants them shipped to Florida."

"How about I deliver them myself. Rather than pay a massive a shipping fee," I offered, "I'd be happy to drive my van for a reimbursement of my expenses."

A trip to Florida, all expenses paid, a good way to see a new part of America I thought. The customer liked the idea and invited me to stay a couple of nights once I arrived.

"Care for a trip to the sun? I need a co-driver." I phoned a friend, Dan.

I couldn't have imagined the shocking insights into American culture I experienced on the trip. I never thought I'd have heard such ignorant racial slurs as I did during those ten days. Late 80s. Unreal, I gasped to Dan, "…and American people are still that racist that they use a derogatory word to describe a customer out loud."

LESSONS ON THE ROAD

After two years in America, a glass of 'red' in my hand, I called a friend, excited I had made two sales.

"I've got to drive my trusty steed to Florida on a delivery trip. Some wealthy clients in Boca Raton will pay my expenses. They've bought two of my 8-foot cut-steel figures. I can't wait to explore more of America." I chit-chatted down the phone to Dan, the divorced ex-husband of my dead girlfriend, Sandra. 'Technically an ex-widower' flashed the thought as I paused to take a sip, 'that is, if such a category existed.'

"How would you like a co-driver?" He volunteered. "I'm desperate to visit one of my girlfriends in Jacksonville. You could drop me off there while you do your business, then collect me on the way home." The receiver vibrated Dan's bedroom intentions over the wire.

And so it was agreed.

"Come dressed warmly," I advised. "The van's no Rolls. But the engine goes like a dream. Does 80s easy."

A rubber mat covered the rust spaces of the floor to keep passengers feet from the hardtop. Blobs of new welding held the roof secure preventing lift-off. A ping-pong ball in the gas tank rattled a warning as it neared empty, its gauge long since defunct. The odometer belied its reading. 'Quirks,' I called them.

As I eased the '79 Dodge Sportsman to a stop in front of Dan's lodgings, he appeared in the doorway, backpack in hand.

"I'm afraid it doesn't open from the outside." I said kicking open the passenger door with my right boot. I swung my red-stockinged leg back over the gear lever and shivered. The chilly blast fanned Dan's corkscrew hair to a wild halo. I smiled, thinking 'if you could only see yourself....'

Dan lived in a mud Hogan he built himself in scrubland beside an arroyo outside Santa Fe with his wife and children. "...to experience how the Navajo live," he deluded himself. But I recalled the harsh reality my friend Sandra, Dan's wife, described, sobbing how she couldn't go on.

"When I weep, or want to be alone, all I can do is face the wall. My only escape are the written pages of the books I keep in an old flour sack."

She stuck it out two years. After they divorced, and my friend died, her neck broken in a crash. In Spain...on a lonely road...at dusk...no seatbelt...her latest lover at the wheel... I pressed my thumb against my forehead, dammed further thoughts.

By the time we pulled into the truck stop in Tyler, Texas, Dan and my stomachs screamed for lunch.

"Is it okay with you if we park amongst the trucks, Dan?" I asked him. "I find them soo... incredibly exciting... all that shiny chrome, those massive wheels, their very size, and their revving and thrumming. We've nothing like them in England."

Like an ant, so small beside the gleaming giants, our paint-stripped van crouched mute while the two of us inside crunched on carrot sticks, and munched egg and cucumber sandwiches. Blowing crumbs, we discussed which of the two lone hitch-hikers waiting on the verge by the exit, we'd offer a ride. The young, long-haired blonde man with a backpack, or the African American wearing a pulled down broad-brimmed country-looking hat leaning on a thick cane who stood surrounded by maybe ten bulging plastic bags?

"If we were to give either of them a ride," I said, "I'd choose the 'country-looking black chappie.' The 'hippie's' bound to be carrying drugs don't you think?" I commented, pigeon-holing both hitchhikers.

Leaving Dan in the van, I gathered our lunch debris into an empty zip-lock bag and headed for the trash and restroom. I lingered in the showroom fingering the trashy goods for sale deciding whether to buy a scorpion trapped in a sand-globe or a coiled plaster rattlesnake ashtray with red bead eyes.

The van's side doors were pulled open and there, peering from under his felt hat, on the back seat sat the African American with all his plastic bags. Startled for a moment, I paused.

"This is Bernard," Dan introduced our passenger. He needs a ride to Alabama … just crooked my finger indicating he could come with us, and Bernard all but flew to jumped inside. So here he is. The poor fellow has been waiting for days."

"Pleased to meet you, ma'am." A smile spread across Bernard's face, then, to my surprise, throwing back his head, raising his eyes and waving both arms, he cried, "Ah noo the Lord would send me someone. Thank you, ma'am. Oh, thank you Lord. Thank you. Hallelujah."

Bernard rode with us for eleven hours. It turned out he was on his way home to see his mother and repay her the money he'd stolen from her cookie jar the year before, when his car had given one last cough then conked out. Dead. The tow truck guy gave him $50, helped him bag all his possessions in plastic and dropped him at the truck stop. But that had been two and a half days ago. Since then, he'd waited hoping for a ride. But nothing. Not one offer. The truck-stop manager began giving him dirty looks, kept coming out, staring to see if he was gone. Bernard went on "…being a 'colored man' and this being Texas…," lynching was on his mind, he told us. "I feared for my life." So he'd moved far from the stop itself to the roadside, and prayed to the Lord, whom he'd recently discovered resided in his soul.

"Saved me. Showed me the way," Bernard concluded. Hence, his repentance for his theft. Hence, his trip to repay his aged ma.

Bernard's hat stayed firmly clamped to his head. His hands gripped the cane propped on the floor between his legs to steady himself. From the back seat, his waterfall of stories spilled over our shoulders egged on by my gasps and genuine 'ooo-ahhs' of wonder. Bernard had been in Vietnam, wounded in the leg. Naïve to the point of stupidity, I exclaimed.

"You never. You actually killed a man?" Bernard gave me a look that said where have you been living…under a gooseberry bush? But he answered me politely,

"A man's life depended on the strength of each member in his foxhole. The weak, we killed. Had to. Relied on one another, see, to watch our backs. Officers, the mean ones disliked by the men, mysteriously disappeared, 'died in combat' shot through the back." Bernard winked knowingly, the sentence trailed unfinished. After the war, when he got back, Bernard confessed like all ex-combatants, he was trigger-happy. Jumpy.

"Yer, sure, I carried a gun." He exclaimed. "Over in 'Nam, slept with one, ate with one. A gun was my third leg. Throw you in the clink not carrying one over there." Bernard paused. "But when I was de-mobbed and back in civvie-street those L.A. cops didn't get it. Locked me up. Slammed me in a mental hospital for 're-acclimatizering,' or something, they called it."

Bernard went on to describe the hospital. "Worse than a prison," he said. "Drugged with pills. Strapped to a bed till *you'se* were a 'good boy.' Zombies, ma'am, that's wha' we was. But I hid them pills, and I found Jesus there. Tha's how I got out."

Whether he escaped or had been pardoned, I didn't care. My brain somersaulted Bernard's war images of swift flashing blades, muffled cries, lethal bullets and barehanded strangulations deep in black foxholes beneath a ground that smelled of blood and death.

Our talk was not entirely of war. We talked of our different lives and accidents of birth. I spoke of India and the Raj, and of the country orphanage where I was raised from six to ten. Dan spoke of growing up as a Jew with his Rabbi Father in New Jersey, and of deliberately provoking him with his rebellious support of the Palestinians and his love of Arab Poetry.

Bernard wouldn't talk much about his childhood. He talked lovingly of the saintly goodness of his ma, and how he'd run away to join up, then taken to drugs, "...that's how we survived that hell, man..." and his shame for stealing from her cookie jar, from his ma who loved him so. I never knew my father, he added.

Bernard and Dan talked about demonstrations for equality for the rights of every American to vote, the discrimination still rife in the South, political stuff that coming from England I was shamefully ignorant of. I listened, my mouth shut. My classroom hummed, alive. The lessons real. Hours passed.

We crossed the state line into either Arkansas, or Louisiana, I don't recall exactly, exited I-40, and pulled into a gas station before heading south on a connecting highway to join Interstate I-10.

"Watch out for the police," the gas-station manager hissed to Dan without elaborating. "Watch out for the po-lice," he repeated, nodding conspiratorially, but refusing to answer Dan's 'what do you mean?'

Dan at the wheel, we'd driven a bare two miles of the twenty, when a police van screamed past us, lights flashing. Another van drew alongside, its side door open, revealed uniformed arms and legs signaling a for us to stop.

"What the devil..." Dan exploded as a third van closed in from the rear. He braked, switched off the ignition. He got out docile, obedient to the chief policeman's demand, while a couple of his henchmen strobed their flashlights along our van's eight-foot-long bed and in through the windows illuminating a forest of tangled metal arms and legs, before focusing one spotlight on Bernard, statue-still on the back seat, and a second on me, seat-belted in the front.

"We intend to search your van. Sir." The chief leered. Prejudice plastered across his forehead.

He'd scored. A weirdly dressed woman in boots, red tights, and a scarlet knee-length sweater decorated with woven fish, a middle-aged man sporting a shock of wild hair, and a 'colored.'

Bernard and I sat expressionless, frozen in our seats, not exchanging glances. Now Dan was a man who'd learned his rights during the riots and demonstrations in the sixties. He spoke deliberately, politely, soothingly calm while looking the policeman in the eye.

"No, Officer. I do not give you permission to search our van. You must have a search warrant, and explain your grounds." Dan paused. "We may look like drug-runners from New Mexico in this beat-up van, but I can assure you, Sir, this respectable lady," he annunciated pointedly, "is delivering sculpture to her clients in Florida, I am the lady's friend and co-driver, and a Senior Lecturer at Rutgers University, and this gentleman," Dan waved, indicating Bernard, "...this gentleman's," again Dan emphasized the word, "... car broke down in Texas, and we are giving him a ride to Montgomery."

Dan stood his ground. Six foot three to the chief's five foot something, his hands in clear view, he stood silent, still, patiently repeating his citizens' rights. Twenty minutes of quietly talking passed before the Chief folded his notebook and tucked it into his upper pocket, then another twenty minutes for him to call off his posse before he waved us on and sped back and away down the narrow lane.

For a moment we didn't move. When Dan finally turned the ignition key, we drove in silence, the engine's hum and the grating gear change the only sound. Dan pulled the van onto the highway spitting expletives.

"Well the manager of the gas station did warn us. He's obviously their stoolie. Told to let the cops know of any unusual travelers. I suppose that could describe us." Dan said.

I looked down and fingered the knitted fish swimming across my chest of the sweater I wore. A fur-lined flying helmet and coils of scarf completed my outfit. Not exactly an all American girl. Conventional, compared to Dan, but definitely strange. Dan's 'afro' hair spoke 'hippie' rather than the Anglo Senior Lecturer of the art department at Rutgers University that he was. And then there was Bernard, of course.

"Yeah." Bernard spoke up, "Dey mean, man. Don't go much for blacks round these parts. Mixing worse, me 'wid' you being a white woman, and you with your afro hair, man. For sure they've planted drugs if they'd searched the van."

Dan added, "Man, that was close. Any excuse to stick a feather in their caps, and prove they were right for stopping us." Dan addressed me, "This isn't England, Liz. No of your cricket rules over here. Whoa. The drug laws here. The bastards could hold us in prison forever in this state."

Whatever knots had held our tongues in check before, freed untied. We howled into silly there-was-once-a...jokes and made up crude limericks using and abusing ourselves and everyone and everything till we ran out of steam. Bernard sang, 'There was a young man of ....' sometimes imitating a southern twang, sometimes with what he labeled a 'black' voice, then 'pinko,' and accents of different states. I attempted and failed to copy him. He did way better imitations than mine. We laughed. We passed around the thermos of coffee. We kept each other awake. Drowsy, we crossed the Mississippi after nightfall. The full moon spread her silver mantle on the water. The world beautiful once more, we revived.

"An' we crothed the Mithithippi by the moonlight," Bernard lisped suddenly wide awake making us fall about laughing.

It was after midnight when the van pulled into Montgomery.

"I can take the bus from here." Bernard said.

Waiting to see our friend off, sleepy, we sat hunched together in the Greyhound bus stop sipping mugs of hot chocolate. Sad it was time to part. Outside, Dan propped my camera atop a folded road map on the hood. The three of us posed, Bernard in the middle holding his cane and with his hat on. Arms about each other, smiling, then flash. For years the snapshot stayed on my fridge recording our bond.

That trip was my anthropology lesson, I'd say relating the story. "It was in late eighties ….I was shocked… prejudice… I first discovered that for some, the great USA was not always the Land of the Free."

Will you be all right now, Bernard? Sure?" I questioned Bernard to cover my sudden pang of parting.

Bernard raised his trouser leg. I gasped. A knife, sheathed, lay strapped to his right leg partly hidden by his sock. "For just in case. You never know." He said.

Dan slipped Bernard $50 for the bus fare, the bus pulled up, he stowed his plastic bags in the hold, he clambered in and Bernard was gone.

Still reeling from my van trip across the country to the tip of Florida, I hungered to see more of America.

Easy, now I had my Green Card in hand, adventure beckoned.

How would you like to be my co-drivers, I invited an artist girlfriend and her new boyfriend. I've heard of a small bronze foundry in Mexico, and would like to check it out.

A few days later I jumped in the car and set off with them for San Miguel de Allende, a two-day drive over the border. Well, I had a good time, but them…? All the two of them wanted was to eat Egg McMuffins and have supper at six. But in Mexico… I began, then shut up. My traveling companions made faces at everything not American.

AIR CONDITIONING

Driving back from San Miguel De Allende, Mexico it was H-O-T. Ninety degrees more or less. The car's a/c kaput, I sprayed myself with water from an emptied *Windex* spray bottle. *Squirt. Squirt.* That felt better. My legs, my thighs, my face and arms dripped. The breeze wafting from the open window over the moisture, cool, delicious.

"Whoa. What the…" I floored the foot brake.

A gang of six armed Federales pointing rifles, bandannas tied around their foreheads stepped from behind some trees and strung themselves across the road forcing me to stop.

"Wake up." I yelled at my co-driver flopped sleeping on the back seat. "It's a holdup."

"Buenas Dias. Que pasa? What's up?" I asked them as pleasantly as I was able as the fatigue-uniformed men approached and grouped around the car.

I'd been warned how sometimes 'Federales' regularly ransomed drivers for money along lonely stretches of highway leading to the U.S. border leaving them stripped half-naked and shoeless on the side of the road without a peso to their name.

The leader jabbed the butt of his rifle through my window. His eyes fixed on my wet thighs and dripping face.

"This doesn't look good," I muttered to my companion forcing a smile.

"Que es esso? What's that?" He menaced jerking the rifle butt towards my spray bottle.

I don't know what possessed me, what made me do it, I suppose it was nervousness, and perhaps to reassure him the wet was only water, harmless, I squirted my face, neck and thighs. *Squirt. Squirt.*

"Es nuestros aire conditional. It's our air conditioning. Quieres algo? Would you like some?" I asked brightly in broken Spanish.

Without waiting for his answer, I aimed the nozzle and squirted his knuckles gripped around the rifle nosed inches from my bare arm.

His gang collapsed, hysterical. The macho leader's mask slipped briefly. He waved us on without demanding my dinero.

Come out to Galisteo next weekend and see our village rodeo, my girl-friend invited. Arriving, I clambered onto the back of her father's weather-beaten pick-up and perched beside on her on the cab for its grandstand view. But for the dust, the cowboy-booted riders and the sting of animal fear in my nostrils, I had to blink that what I was seeing was no movie, but real.

Hi, David. I'd like to introduce you to my English friend. My girlfriend greeted a village neighbor appearing from a crowd of her friends. And there below me, staring from beneath a wide-brimmed felt hat, a man's, a handsome man's, eyes caught mine.

Hi, Liz, he said. *Why don't you come down here and let me show you the bulls. It's a much better view from ground level.*

I liked his smile, the solid look of him, the blueness of his eyes, the tingle his voice invoked someplace below my ribs.

Taking his outstretched hand, I jumped down from the truck bed almost falling into his arms.

*Be nice to my English friend, my girlfriend threat-
ened as David, her doctor friend, lead me away.
And over the next I months he was. Nice. Super
nice, to be more accurate. I, he, we, fell in love.*

*Let's take a camping trip to Canyon de Chelly
next weekend, David suggested, dates later. A
few days together will be a good way to see if we
get along.*

*I even have a tent, I replied seeing myself already
naked beside him enfolded in a sleeping bag.
Sunsets. Moonlight. I could hardly wait.*

LIES STREAMING

I'm not a liar by nature, so I was sort of shocked to hear myself telling such an outright whopper. Even as the lie tumbled from me, I was aware I was lying. I had never actually assembled that particular, that very tent, as I swore I had in answer to my new boyfriend's question, "Do you know how to put up *this* tent? Have you put this tent up before?" He asked emphasizing this, and wanting to please him, I blithely nodded, hoping that a nod did not qualify as a lie. 'And after all,' I convinced myself, 'a tent's a tent. What could be so difficult to fathom, what could be so different to the 6x6 foot tent I and my previous husband, had put up for years in Spain and the dome tent for my boys exactly like the present one I'd pulled from the garage to show him, apart from the color being blue that is, while the first was a leafy green?'

We, my new boyfriend and I, were at that point in our relationship of putting ourselves in all kinds of situations to discover how *un* or how *com*-patible we were. We'd survived many journeys on the road, and once driven two and a half days over the border to San Miguel de Allende and marveled at the clusters of orange Monarch butterflies that transformed the trees to flaming pyramids, but now it was time for a greater test, the test of camping, which I have to say sounds more romantic than it often is.

In our case, we packed the car and drove to Canyon de Chelly singing. That's was before the trouble started. Once the tent site had been carefully chosen on a pancake-flat rectangle of ground close to a cluster of Rabbit Bush, 'handy to pee behind,' we decided cheerfully, for we were still cheerful at that point stretching and pegging out the ground sheet and spreading the nylon fly facing East so we would see the rising sun through the flap. Next, we lined up the tent poles on the ground in neat rows. So far so good, but it was time then to snap the sectioned rods straight and insert them through the loops of the dome's seams and fit the rod ends' one into the other. Well, that is what should have happened, but by then I was wishing they'd been numbered, the poles I mean, along with a manual of simple 1-2-3 steps, for clearly the poles had grown too long and however forcefully we tried, and my boyfriend was a big man sort of like Popeye after he's consumed a mound of spinach, it became clear as day, although it was getting dark by then, that even he, my trial fiancé with all his strength had failed. One look at his face and I knew I'd better do something fast to unclamp his hard-set lips, and needed to act that minute to avoid the catastrophe that loomed, but had not yet quite fallen, if you get my meaning. Quick as a flash, I snapped open a folding chair, turned it to view the setting sun, back towards me so he wouldn't watch, and thrust a chigger of neat Tequila in his hands saying as calmly as I could, "Here, sit here. Enjoy a drink. I'll get the damn thing up, no worries."

With neither his strength or notion how, I did, I fixed it, I tied the poles criss-crossed together as I'd seen lodge-poles of a teepee in grainy movies, which made the inside a little strange considering it was supposed to be a dome tent. Round. But the thing was up. That's all I cared, and after a couple of stiff margaritas, my boyfriend didn't care either.

We only camped that one night. Next day we checked into a motel.

That did it for camping. No more tents for us. Ever. Having survived the near disastrous hiccup thanks to my, well, I confess, big lie, for our next getaway, we rented a one-room mountain log and chink cabin outside the old mining town of Creed, Colorado. With enough food and booze in the cool box for ten days, we holed up in self-imposed isolation with only chipmunks and wild birds for company.

Day, night, breakfast on the porch, evenings bathed in shared silence our pencils captured images and dreams. We had no reason to emerge. Packed up, the car loaded, we turned in the cabin key and bumped the dirt road to Creed's mining town and back to civilization.

Human music spilling from a jute box, the clink of coins, crunch of boot on blackened pine wood floor, chatter, strike of match, we stood dazed sipping a beer at one end of a dimly lit cowboy bar. Not intentionally, not craning to catch their words, we couldn't help but eavesdrop the laughter and story being shared between the two cowboy-hatted, and silver belted cow-hands lounging at the far end of the polished bar downing shots of bourbon.

Neither David or I moved. Neither of us breathed till finally the telling of the tale came to an end. Mentally, scribbling down every word, I changed nothing.

BOOBY TRAP

Jim checked his log cabin in the Pecos Wilderness. Yes, everything was in its place, the woodstove emptied of ash, taps run dry, and every mouse, and bear-attracting crumb bagged and buried by the dead Douglas pine on the edge of his land. From that very spot in front of the sink, he witnessed the tree's life struck from its limbs in a blinding instant four summers back. He left its leafless, silvery-grey skeleton standing. 'An icon to the suddenness of death,' by his way of thinking.

Jim drew the gingham curtains along the length of twine that served as a rail.

"Damn. Blast it." He thumped his fist onto the paint-chipped kitchen table. "I'll show you sons of bitches."

His Blue Heeler, Mr. Pepper, sat up, cocked an ear enquiringly at Jim. They spent their summers up in Jim's grandfather's cabin in the woods, Mr. Pepper and him.

Jim saw himself knee-high, standing before his Gran'pa's rocking chair on the wooden porch and listening to him recount stories of his past. He smelled again the acrid 'baccy' lingering in his nostrils from the pipe Gran'pa'd whittled with his own two hands. After his dad died, Jim was alone. His ma's face had long since faded.

"'Nough of reminiscing, Mr. P. Time to get to business." Jim fetched the broom, swept the last cloud of dust through the open door, and pulled it shut. He turned the key and put it in his backpack.

Every year before the first snows fell, Jim abandoned his cabin for the winter leaving it locked and clean ready for the next summer. For the past six years, vandals had broken in leaving a mess of open cans and dirty plates. Jim reddened at the ugly memory.

He reached for his shotgun, dropped a cartridge down the barrel, snapped it shut, and strapped it to the back of a kitchen chair with the stock propped on the table. Bending down, one eye closed, Jim sighted the barrel aiming it at the front door. Unrolling a ball of string, he looped one end to the old-fashioned iron door latch, and tied the other to the trigger.

"Try breaking in now, you buggers." Jim smiled, carefully releasing the safety catch.

With one last look at his handiwork, Jim dropped his pack, followed by Mr. Pepper and lastly himself out of the window, then, nailed it shut. Once on the ground, he pulled on his wide-brimmed hat.

"Let's hit the road, Mr. Pepper." He whistled, "Come." And together they headed down the mountain to winter in town.

Next spring when the sun was warm, as was his habit, Jim and Mr. Pepper retraced their steps to summer in the cabin. As he walked, he busied his head with plans—*extend the clearing, fence a patch against the mule deer, perhaps, plant some corn…* He was happy.

"We're home, Mr. Pepper."

Jim put the key in the lock and pushed. *Boooom.* Jim fell to the ground clutching his chest.

Travel. It became a pattern, David's, me as a tag-a-long, for it was he who paid. Chose a different place to escape the winters. Trinidad and Tobago came next. My Guyanese girlfriend mentioned her barrister cousin, Vernon, lived in Trinidad, and although perfect strangers to him, he agreed for us to stay.

WELCOME LIZ AND DAVID without that sign we'd be still searching for Vernon in that swirling airport crowd of maybe 500 expectant people.

A bed, books and papers stacked high on the floor, dust, blood splats of deceased mosquitoes…It's like the house of Mr. Biswas, I whispered as we retired into his back-bedroom to unpack.

Rum, rum, and more rum loosened our tongues, and by the end of the first evening we were the best of friends. An open house, his friends came and went.

Back by two, Vernon would call, and leaving for his office each morning, turning the key locked us inside his house. Kidnappers, armed robbers, he explained…Too dangerous for you to wander around by yourselves."

We were never bored. His housekeeper kept us busy in the kitchen. From her we learned to mix, roll, and make lentil-stuffed chapattis to serve with the curries she served us.

"I'm back. Ready to explore?" Vernon would call.

Making up for the lost morning, Vernon crammed the afternoon and evening with outings to his favorite places. Ominous, bubbling, a lake of molten pitch; another time, the never to be for-gotten returning flocks of scarlet ibis roosting on a rock island transforming it to a flaming cone… Did Vernon ever sleep?

Once home and lounging barefoot in his living room, then followed a game of chess, or cards, and talk, talk, talk. Rum-fueled, far into the night he kept us up with philosophical wisdoms long forgotten.

Carnival, Jump-up time, Trinidad's entire population crammed the streets for the celebration. Vernon dressed us up as Rainbows. And Jump-up we did.

Rum the only liquid available in the hot sun, we bumped and ground beside near naked revelers to the crash of steel bands from eight in the morning to after midnight.

Till next time, both Vernon and we sadly waved when we parted. Promises. Intentions. Christmas Cards, and the occasional phone call we nursed our connection, but never did we meet in person again.

VERNON'S PICNIC

Pongal, the Hindu Harvest Festival celebrated each year in Trinidad fell while David and I were holidaying there.

Our Lawyer friend and host, Vernon, knocked on our bedroom door before breakfast.

"Come," he said, "I've arranged a beach picnic to meet a few friends on the Indian Beach, the far side of the island. We should leave soon.

Indian? Vernon, being Indian himself, his epitaph surprised me.

A 'few friends' turned out to be fifty. Picnic, an all-day curry-fest prepared and cooked from scratch. The beach seethed by the time we arrived, every close parking spot occupied, we parked above the palm-fringed bay high on the cliff.

Burdened with crates of beer, we staggered from the road to join Vernon's friends; women, already busy peeling, chopping; men, busy popping beer bottles, sharpening knives, building fires. Vernon and a friend made for the jungle carrying machetes, and returned dragging dead fronds of palm and banana.

Green-mango curry, chicken coconut, snake-gourd, ginger seer fish, dhal, and vegetable curries bubbled and browned over the fires, and later in our bellies.

David and I pulled off our shirts to swim, and wished I hadn't. I looked so naked, so white beside the sun-darkened Indian browns, and women paddling modestly in their saris. Squealing children ran at us laughing and smacking the waves. David flopped up and down in the shallows like a mighty whale splashing after them.

Picnickers sprawled in siesta poses crowding every patch of shade. I lolled propped against a palm mesmerized by moving shadow lines cast by its leaves, my eyes lazily sweeping the ocean below the blinding sun suspended above the horizon. Sunset wouldn't be long.

"Hey look. That's odd," I exclaimed. "Won't that boat's keel get stuck in the sand coming in so close?"

Beyond the breakers, a yacht in full sail appeared headed fast for shore. I shaded my eyes. A rubber dinghy trailed from her stern. The yacht gleamed pristine white dressed with a navy-blue plimsol line. Streamlined. Venezuela's pennant fluttered from her mast alongside Trinidad's diagonally striped black on red. No crew scurried on deck. No navigator steered at the helm. No Captain bellowed orders. Horror. Her bow reared from the water revealing her belly. Smack. She dropped splintering the spume. A wave sloshed across her bows flooding the deck. Swimmers scrambled from the sea. People on the beach, pointing, gathering in groups, called their children.

Five men waded to chest height grabbing uselessly for a handhold.

"Ahoy there. Anybody?" Their voices rippled with the tide, and back out again to sea.

"Watch out. Mind your heads," the beach crowd yelled.

In the nick of time, the five men dove, ducking as the masts' boom swung back and forth in wild sweeps over the sea, jib and ropes flapping narrowly missing the men. Bow pointing, foaming surf rolled her onto her starboard hull she almost capsized. The next breaker lifted her sideways and beached her in three feet of water. She lay there tilted on her side, her sails floating uselessly on the sea's surface.

The crowd surged, then froze. A man's body slithered off the sloping deck and vanished with a splash. A weighted package followed sinking from sight.

"Keep back. Step away." A posse of armed police burst from the trees behind us.

Whistles shrilled. Guns pop-popped. Staccato screams scorched the air. Every picnicker flung face down in the sand.

Next day's Herald's headlines read; "Drug Lord's body recovered with 100 pound of Cocaine."

Venturing farther afield we traced our fingers along the indented coast of the Eastern seaboard. Belize, we chorused jabbing the map. How about snorkeling in the famed azure seas? A week later we checked into a thatched palapa at what should have been an idyllic beach resort. Five days straight, apart from mad dashes to the restaurant, torrential rain kept us imprisoned indoors. Disaster.

Drip drip, the rain sent us crazed.

WISH YOU WERE HERE

"Enough. I'm for getting the hell out of here. Today. Coming with me?" It wasn't a question.

Grim faced, my boyfriend, David, glanced up from the third book he'd glowered through during the past five day listening to the incessant rain drip-dripping through the straw roof of our Belize Palapa to puddle on the dirt floor.

Unable to scuba dive, or laze the beach as planned, leaving for Guatemala a week earlier was no great loss. The one dive we made our first day had put me off diving for life. Struggling against a low rip tide fifteen feet down along the seabed and coming face to face with a moray eel peering menacingly at me from his rock cave was not for me, I had secretly decided.

"Good idea. I'm all for it," I agreed enthusiastically.

David vanished into the downpour headed for the airstrip, reappearing within fifteen minutes triumphant,

"Scored two singles, on the only flights out to the mainland that day," he beamed. "The flights are only four hours apart. Which do you prefer? First or second?"

"You go first. I'll wait here where I feel safe."

"See you in Belize City in four hours." Loaded down with now our useless scuba gear David was gone.

Four hours later the six-seater plane rose from the rain-soaked landing strip for the fifteen-minute flight and dropped me onto the tarmac of Belize city.

"Taxi's waiting. If we hurry, we'll just make the bus." David hustled me into a beaten-up low-rider, where a man in a torn undershirt waited at the wheel.

"This a taxi?" I hesitated to get in.

The taxi driver deposited us at a grimy diesel-filled garage. "This? The Bus Station, really?" I checked, unsure. "Yes. Yes. Guatemala bus," the driver pointed to an unmarked tube on wheels.

Scrambling to stow our luggage, David and I slid onto a metal seat for the seven-hour ride to the Guatemalan border.

We had no visa. We didn't know we needed one. "Last week they refused entry to a man because he was British" A fellow traveler cheerily informed us.

"Frontera. All out," the bus driver gesticulated, when at last the bus rattled to a stop.

I stared though the glassless window. It was almost dusk.

"Just look confident," David muttered.

The two Immigration officials in the guardhouse were too engrossed playing cards to give us a second glace.

"Buenas Tardes," I smiled faking an American accent hoping to fool them I was any nationality but British.

VISA. 28 DAYS. Without looking up, they stamped both passports. We, our snorkeling gear and luggage, were through. The jungle border-crossing was just that, a crossing into the jungle. No Buses, no taxi-stand, no hotel, no official to advise us. We hesitated perplexed.

"Donde es el hotel?" To my growing horror, the stranger shook his head but he pointed down the street and I gathered the one and only taxi-driver rented rooms.

Leaving David minding our snorkeling gear and many bags, I set off along the wide dirt track between two rows of crude cement-block buildings with barred windows hoping it was safe for me, an anglo woman, to be walking alone only to be startled by a piglet-sized rat scuttling beside me.

I earned some odd looks, hurrying in the dusk calling 'Donde esta la casa de…?' till I found the taxi driver's house. 'No taxi hoy. Manana, taxi,' he said, but for $2 we could spend the night, and for $60 he'd drive us to Tikal the next day.

The barred room he showed us with its two iron cots was the size of a prison cell. We shared the basic 'facilities' down a narrow passage with other inmates.

"What time want taxi?" He inquired.

"What time you start? 5am? Perfecto," I fired back.

"Isn't that a little early?" David queried, surprised.

"You surely don't think we'll sleep do you?" I responded pointing to two armed guards stationed outside our barred cell to protect us. "…and with all these mosquitoes?"

At dawn we found a middle-aged woman already sitting in the front passenger seat when we clambered into the back. "My wife, Concha like come with me. Okay?" Our taximan-host introduced her.

Tikal's archaeological site lay sixty miles along a rough unpaved track into the deep jungle of All Spice, Ceiba and other majestic trees. About two hours into our journey, the taxi shuddered to a stop as a group of armed youths in their teens and twenties, sprung from the undergrowth barring the track, rifles pointed at the windscreen.

"Hola. Buen dia. Que pasa?" I smiled innocently.

It wasn't until they allowed us to pass and our driver started shaking, I realized the hold-up was no playact, and we'd narrowly escaped being killed, robbed or taken hostage.

Tikal's ruins rose welcomely above the jungle. For $40 each we could sleep on a mattress in a hall with twenty other tourists, an Official smiled. One look at the row of basins sporting twenty toothbrushes convinced us to continue on to the neighboring town of Flores ten miles down the road.

We booked into a Japanese-style resort built on stilts over the water. The first evening I slid into the lake for a gloriously refreshing dip.

"I wouldn't go in the water." An American fellow guest advised the following morning before my breakfast swim.

"You don't want to know," is all he'd answer to my 'why ever not' response, until I threatened. "Unless you tell me, I'm going to go."

"Crocodiles. Under the jetty. Just where you were swimming last evening."

I remained on dry land after that. David too and we spent our days wandering Tikal's mysterious ruins, and exploring an island village to photograph the rare dugouts still used to traverse the waters by the Indigenous Indians. Lunch called.

"That place looks nice. There under the trees," we pointed selecting one of several tin shacks.

Studying the maze of mystery dishes illustrated with pictures and descriptions of the creatures we could eat, I chose a long-tailed tree animal with an unpronounceable name similar to 'Texipinkle, that hopefully dined healthily on fruit and leaves. It was delicious. We were both still adventurous then and not yet vegetarian.

"Phew. God, I smell awful." I sniffed later that evening plucking at my T-shirt and fanning air towards my armpits.

For the two remaining days in Flores, David wouldn't, couldn't come near me and held his nose. I couldn't bear to be with me either. My reeking self followed me everywhere I went.

To get back on track with our original itinerary, we hopped on a plane to Guatemala.

No working seat belts or catches on the overhead bins to keep them from flying open, clutching the back of the seat I prayed the lumbering plane wouldn't fall apart before we landed in Guatemala City.

Too many machine-gunned bullet holes still scarred the walls, too much blood scrubbed invisible but still palpable, and too many desperate poor. For the first time, I feared for our safety. Driving through a market, a mob swarmed the taxi hammering on the windows forcing us to stop. The poverty-stricken city was no place for us gringos to hang around.

Next stop, Lake Atitlan, a second-rate hotel perched its banks. The sunset blazed glorious before the darkening quiet. Through the high window facing into the hall a flashing light beamed into our room. We lay awake. Fitfully slept. Opening my eyes at dawn, I startled to see David standing fully clothed with his suitcase in hand.

"I don't know about you," he growled, "but I'm not spending a night like that again. But coming or not, I'm, leaving today." I left with him.

Did we drive? Did we go by taxi? I can't recall, but the drive took us to the top of a mountain to Chichicastenango, famed for its native market and Holy Church.

Finally, something magical about our holiday. Red, yellow, pink and orange, Gladioli strew the steps of St. Thomas Church. Hymns to God, and swirling incense and candlelight cocooned us in a vaulted world as we prayed beside the local people. A young girl, no more than six, led her grandmother by the hand as she slowly inched the painful distance to the altar on her knees. A man offered up a live chicken. He rubbed its beak along the stone altar step and it fell unconscious in a trance. The women peeked at us from beneath their mantillas, giggling at David sittting with me on the women's side.

Our hotel, a hacienda, an island in an ocean milling with coconut-oiled hair. A smiling Guatemalan dressed in a traditional white kilt, a tasseled cap, with scarlet strapping criss-crossed about his legs, stood bare-footed outside our brass studded door all night to feed the fire in our room when it died low. We dined on exquisite French cuisine prepared by a French chef, we sipped French wine, and escaped the claustrophobic jostling market in the street by resting in the hacienda's flower-filled courtyards.

"Merci, Madame." We thanked its French owner.

We should have stayed.

I admit it. I am stubborn. Despite all the warnings to the contrary, I insisted we go to the sea. "The seaside and beaches are always special." And this one was. Against David's better judgment, he rented a jeep. Seven hours later, the coast hove in sight. Tin hovels, temporary dwellings for the unfortunate, littered trash and dirt made it clear that to stay was to invite a violent end. Panicked now, I scoured the map. "Only seventy-five more miles. See here, RESORT. Its clearly marked."

Encouragingly the sign proclaimed it did exist. We had arrived at last. A group of buildings huddled on higher ground overlooking the beach. It was in the middle of a dry lake. We parked the jeep and froze stock-still mid-bridge leading to the entrance. Two armed men running towards us rattled bullets over the parapet into the moat.

Rats. Thank the Lord. Not us, their targets were rats.

"Its closed for the season." The men told us. "But for $75 we let you stay."

Three rooms later, we found one with a door that locked, a window that opened, a working toilet, and a shower with running water. It was fine for one night to regroup,

It was hot. I changed into my bikini to drown my guilt and disappointment in the swimming pool. Looking at the lurid green water, David refused to put in a toe. Not me, I jumped. Cool, I wanted cool. As I surfaced, I came face to face with large, black, pincered creatures swimming with me in the pool. Out! I was out so fast I flew.

Not even the line of pink flamingos low over the darkening sea against a blazing sky on fire, could quench my husband's fury, or expunge my guilt. So angry was our silent drive back to Guatemala City for the flight home, that one mighty lurch and bump over a pothole clicked my crooked vertebra in place, and set me laughing like a crazed hyena.

We mailed our holiday postcards. "Wish you were here."

Not all our holidays were as disastrous. We traveled many places both within and beyond the United States. Italy, Chile, Scotland, France, the globe became ours. We rented a cabin for $30 on Costa Rica's black sands where we sketched datura blossom and walked the shore together under blazing scarlet skies. David tying a bandanna around his head, dressed in only a sarong, wore a scarlet hibiscus blossom behind one ear and smiled the entire holiday. He smiled again when he turned fifty.

THE BIG 5-0

"Rather a lot of food just for the two of us, isn't it?" Puzzled, Lisa's lover stepping through the front door glanced around the casita searching for, but not finding the expected candlelight dinner table set for just the two of them. Sushi rolls spilled from dishes among chaotic stacks of blue plastic plates, cutlery, chopsticks and glasses covered the kitchen table.

"Umm, well, actually..." Saved from answering, Lisa turned as the front door pushed open.

"Hi. Nice seeing you. It's been too long," an artist friend announced stepping inside unbuttoning his coat. "Shall I dump my things in the bedroom?"

The front doorbell rang again followed by a stream of icy air as the door swung ajar. Lisa's lover frowned, his eyebrows lifted seeing two of his doctor colleagues enter, unwinding scarves and shaking off the frost sprinkled on their woolen hats.

"Brrr. Bloody cold out there." Pulling off their gloves, they handed Lisa a be-ribboned bottle.

Open. Shut. Again. Open. Another friend. Another bottle. More happy 50th old man birthday cards.

"I get it..." Lisa's lover sighed, shaking his head. "I'm not the only one invited." Pouring himself a glass of Pinot Noir he broke into a smile.

Though no one said "Surprise, David" Lisa could tell it was. Lisa's lover turned the Big 5-0 that week. Worth a celebration, Lisa thought laying her plans. Pictured a belly dancer. A triple chocolate birthday cake with fifty flaming candles on her head.

Soon, twenty plus friends crowded the casita. Like chickens in their coop, they pecked and drank and squawked, happy with their feasting.

"Did you see his face? He didn't, and doesn't suspect a thing." Lisa and a girlfriend whispered giggling in the kitchen as they cleared the decks, collected debris.

The door-bell rang though only Lisa heard. A woman shrouded beneath a hooded cape, and her husband carrying a boombox stood illuminated in the doorway.

"Shh, come in, come in," Lisa beckoned ushering them inside.

Ta-Da….a crash of cymbals. Music crescendoed. Lights dimmed. The room hushed. "Take your places," the stranger's husband called.

Expectant, Lisa's guests settled on the banco along the two adjacent walls, on the floor, finding room where they could.

A wail of Middle Eastern music filled the room and a barefoot woman slithered from the dark. On her head fifty candles flamed atop an iced chocolate cake, just as Lisa dreamed.

Jeweled belly-button shaking, hips undulating, gold-tasseled brassiere jiggling, twirling, she, the blonde belly-dancer danced her way around the room and with an alluring shake of her breasts, stopped before the birthday boy. Once, twice, three times, she circumvented the room, bells tinkling, inviting dollar bills from the cheering guests. "Here. Stuff the bills here," enticed the hip-band encircling the dancer's proffered expanse of belly flesh.

No encore. No fourth circle. She ignored the clapping. Candles extinguished, her husband hovered, hawk-eyed his watch, announced wordlessly. We've done what we were paid to do. Now it was time to go. He pocketed her pay, folded her dollar bills and whisked her out into the night. Stunned. Subdued, the guests never moved. Sat silent.

"That was it? Just that? Three circuits?" Cheated, Lisa's blood rose up. Her face flushed. "Okay. Bugger that. Anybody want to belly dance? If not, then I will."

Lisa, stood, pushed her skirt below her waist, unpinned her hair.

"Lisa. Lisa….," the guests whistled. Music. Music, they clapped till someone turned on the record player.

Head back, hips, breasts and belly quivering, a cobra, Lisa's body snaked, hypnotized the seated guests.

Fun and laughter. Wine flowed. No ice remained. Midnight came and went. Wined and dined, guests departed. Good party. Happy 50th David.

Alone together at last, sleep descended on Lisa and Lisa's lover.

Next morning Lisa crawled from bed. Strewn clothes littered the floor and all around a scattering of dollar bills, ones, more ones, twenties, fives and tens.

"What the devil?" Lisa exclaimed. "It was a good party. I remember the belly dancer but…me…?" Lisa bit her lip and blushed.

Then it was—Lisa remembered.

I'd like to have met your parents," I said to David on that nine-hour to Phoenix airport to pick up my son Miles and his family.

"You wouldn't have liked him, and as a strict orthodox Jew, they would never have agreed to ever meet you. In the four years we were married, neither my father or my mother once spoke to my ex. Manny was my father's name. Mean as they come." David related. "Dad used to chase me down the street flailing his belt trying to whack me. Usually I was too fast." David, shook his head.

"I have one funny story about him, though" Swearing he hadn't made the story up.

As usual, Saturdays and Sundays Manny put my brother and me to work in the Dry Goods store he owned. Unpaid, of course." David smiled as he began.

THE SALESMAN

Harold patted the crown of his Homburg, turned up the black Astrakhan collar of his coat, and with a quick check at his image in the hall mirror, called, "Goodbye Ethel, dear. Back around six," and with a bang of the front door was gone.

Harold crossed the street to the market in Windsor, Ontario, to a large open-sided space between Mrs. B's cheese stall and the New York Deli.

"Morning, Arnie. Morning, Bert. Good day, Mrs. B." Harold greeted all the stall-holders by name.

Passing Mr. Samon's fish stall, instead of trotting out his daily joke, 'Got any salmon, Mr. Samon?' He called, "keep me a nice piece of your Pike. Enough for three. My doctor son's home for the weekend." That evening he wanted to celebrate.

It was still early but many fruit and vegetable stalls were in full swing and the floor already strewn with stalks, beetroot leaves, cauliflower trimmings, carrot tops, and onionskins. Harold sniffed, delighting in the heavy odor.

'Harold's Dry Goods.' Harold bent, freed the padlock bolting the metal grill to the floor, rolled it up just enough to step inside then, lowered it behind him. Its clatter prepped him for his day. He felt his way through the dark shop to a glass cubicle at the back, and only then turned on the light, and only then once inside his cubicle.

Harold treasured the hour before opening. His hour. He unbuttoned his coat, squared it straight on its hanger, and hung his Homburg on the Bentwood rack. Taking a small bottle of milk from the left pocket, he placed it on the speckled green Formica table beside a jar of sugar, one spoon, four cups and saucers, and a tin of sweet Huntley and Palmer biscuits. Ethel hated waste and sent him off with just enough milk for six cups of tea. Two for him, two for Brian and a little over just in case. He rummaged for the matches and lit the gas ring.

Seated at his Roll-top Desk, Harold opened a large red, inventory ledger. Though nothing had changed overnight, checking every item was a ritual he enjoyed. Harold sold menswear only, work clothes, sizes S, M, L, XL and XXL, heavy boots and plain lace-up shoes. He ran his pencil down the list. 3 dozen. Overalls: brown. Coats: navy. Coats: black. Plaid wool shirts: green, red and blue. Then socks and slippers, rain gear and caps, Harold could almost list the stock from memory. His pencil paused. Boots, 15 Pr. Size 12. Left foot only.

Every year for the past fifteen years, a man with a left clubfoot bought one boot, the right boot. 'Paid full price too,' Harold had smugly told his son when he'd tried to chuck the left one out, 'mark my words, a man will come in one day wanting just the left boot. You wait and see.' And so, multiplying boot by boot, they'd gathered dust out of sight on the highest shelf.

The rattle of the metal grill rolling back told Harold his private hour was up.

"Just me, Mr. Harold." His assistant called, and flipping all four switches illuminated the shop from front to back one sixty-watt bulb at a time. 'Enough for the customers to see without being blinded,' Harold had declared, though Brian would have preferred more wattage, say seventy-five.

"It's going to be a splendid selling day today, Brian."

"Oh yes indeed Sir, Mr. Harold."

Brian sold socks, and handkerchiefs and other small items to the first customers. One XXL sized man bought a red plaid wool shirt. Harold recorded each sale carefully in the ledger before impaling the receipt-slip on a spike.

Mid-morning came around.

"Take a break Brian. Put on the kettle. I'll mind the stall."

As Harold moved from the cubicle to the floor, a man walked slowly by, stopped, turned back and limped in.

Before Harold had time to ask, 'May I help you, Sir?' The man inquired, "Can you oblige? I want a pair of work boots, size 12," and plumped himself down on one of the three chairs Harold kept for his customers.

It was then, when the man sat down, Harold noticed. The man had a wooden leg to which was attached a boot, a right boot. His pulse rate jumped. He flushed.

"Will Sir be needing both boots, or merely the left?" Harold controlled his expression, as though having a wooden leg, a right wooden leg was the most normal thing in all the world.

Back in the stock room he called, "Quick. Hurry. Brian, size twelve, the left boots from the top shelf.

Harold carried a sample brown, and a black one to the front. He knelt.

"Perhaps one of these, Sir?" Harold's hand fumbled with the laces.

The fit was perfect. The price was right. Harold sold all fifteen left boots to the one-legged man, the man with the wooden leg.

Triumphant, too excited to work, Harold left work early that day leaving Brian to close up shop. His doctor son had already arrived home, and was talking animatedly to his mother, Ethel about blood work and hemoglobin counts. Harold bided his time. While the Pike was baking, he poured three glasses of the homemade plum brandy he'd made from the pure alcohol he'd once badgered from his son.

"Both of you, come sit down. I have something to celebrate,"

Harold picked up a knife from the set table and dinged his glass.

"You'll never believe it…," he began. Looking at his audience, Harold related the day, adding. "I doubled my money." His face glowed. "…and for full price too."

*Itchy feet. Doctor David loved to travel. France!
Yes Nice. He'd take me there for a month. So we
could brush up on our French we signed up for
two weeks French school.*

PHOTOGRAPH

Glancing up, (did he count our wrinkles to assess our ages?) The man in Nice's tourist office informed us we qualified for a Senior Citizen's travel pass. Handing us a map, he marked the spot.

"Ici. Pension Office for your travel pass."

The day was warm—delicious. Winter's ice and snow left far behind at home, we dawdled, stopping at a 'tabac' to sit—as much to savor the sun as for 'un café noir.'

Then on we rambled through the winding streets until we tracked down the Pension Office on a back street corner.

We joined the line shuffling forward towards the front.

"You'll both need photographs." The assistant passed over two forms without looking up. "Next?"

Dismissed, we left. Now where to get a photo was the question?

"The Station. It'll have a booth." We were right, they did.

David spoke the better French, so went first. He closed the curtain, and followed the instructions dropping the requisite coins in the appropriate slots. He pressed the buttons; Un. Deux. Trois. Smile.… Stiff, he posed. Waited. The flash never flashed. Precious change-coins so carefully selected, cascaded loudly from the reject slot. "Must have pressed the wrong button. I'll try again." The second time, a flash, a blank white paper and no money returned.

Giving up, we set off on our search for another booth. Signs along the station's busy road, tired sex shops flashed 'le show' to lure the desperate. Not a booth in sight, we scurried by.

"Le super…Là. Là." There, a passerby directed us to a store. "Top end of the street. 'À la gauche,' to the left. Photo booth."

We found it in the super as he said, its curtain taped shut. OUT OF ORDER, a hand scrawled notice declared.

My feet ached, the pavements hardened in the beating sun. I was all for giving up. But there it was—another booth close to the bus stop. Operational, it rewarded our quest with photographs. Triumphant, we returned to the Pension Office, paid the ten-euro fee and fled outside, our senior travel-passes in hand.

Hurrying for a trolley-bus, David and I hopped aboard, held my pass to the scanner. Opening his for the scanner to read, he gasped.

"Bbb…but it's blank. The bloody thing has no photo," he stuttered.

Sightless, the auto-scanner read his photo-less pass and spat out a ticket as though his face was there.

"See, you'll be OK," I assured. "You've proof of payment, don't worry."

But my husband obsessed. Arrest, fines, deportation even, he just had to get a photograph. Our bus expeditions to Eze, Juan les Pins, and Valuris, and trains to Frejus and Cannes, were colored by our hunts to find a working photo booth.

One outing, two weeks later, stepping from the train at Antibes, I spied it.

"There David. Look a booth."

He drew the curtain. Smoothed his hair. Sat. Followed the French instructions.

"Success," he shouted as the machine ate every coin flashed.

A whirring followed. Regurgitated a photo.

"At last. Hurrah," we cried snatching the photo as it slipped from the slot."Whaaaaa," we screeched, gawping.

The image displayed my husband as a bearded blond crowned

with flowing locks and drooped moustache.

Too angry to laugh, he tore it up. Confetti-sized shiny scraps fluttered to the tracks.

I've always regretted not keeping the photo as a memento. I wish we had kept it.

How about getting away for Thanksgiving this year. England maybe?

Let's, I replied scouring google search. That's a fabulous idea.

England: Dorset cottage nestled in country lane: thatched roof, baby-blue framed windows: open wood fire: walking distance to historic wishing well, and ancient Roman Encampment.

Sounded perfect. What more could we ask?

We snapped it up.

THANKSGIVING IN FOREIGN PARTS

On a years' sabbatical, David and I rented a thatched cottage in Dorset, England. Thanksgiving loomed. A peat fire blazed. The chintz curtains, drawn, the two of us sat reading in the oak-beamed living room.

"Let's do a traditional Thanksgiving, but English Christmas style."

Glancing up from Mrs Beaton's, a massive 100-page recipe tome on household management written in the 1800s, I'd discovered on the kitchen shelf, I broke the cozy silence.

And so it was, Saturday, next, we drove to Dorchester's weekly Farmers' Market to select our turkey—live—from the gobbling selection of birds arraigned in wooden coops.

Place your hand on the bird's breast. Pinch. It should feel nicely plump. I quoted aloud from Mrs .B's.

David pushed his hand between the narrow slats and weighed the bird with his palm.

"This one," he declared.

We looked away while the stallholder gripped the bird's neck in a bootjack, as with one yank, the poor thing met its end.

Money exchanged, David took possession, gingerly carrying our Thanksgiving bird by the twine binding its feet.

Wandering the stalls, brussel-sprouts, parsnips, onions, potatoes, sweet chestnuts in their skins, a bunch each of parsley and sage made it to our baskets. And from the produce stall, added farm-fresh butter and milk for bread sauce, sausage meat for stuffing.

"Now for a slab of Stilton cheese. According to Mrs. B, serving cheese as an alternative to brandy butter is a must and "should be eaten with the final course of fruit mince-pies after flambéed Plum Pudding along with assorted crystallized fruit.""

Luckily seven days remained for preparation. Back at the cottage, guts, feathers and all, we strung the bird upside down.

"Hanging for at least a week prior to eating, tenderizes the meat," Mrs. Beaton instructed.

"No way," I remonstrated. "Tomorrow, it's de-gut and feather, or I shan't touch the thing."

Day two. Tackle bird.: pluck and gut.

Outside the back door, David pulled feathers, plucking the bird naked enough to gut. My job—boiling water.

"Phew." The smelly job is best un-described. Save the liver, neck and 'lights' for gravy. Remove feet. That we did easily, but somehow, we skipped the sentence, "AND …make sure to pull out both leg tendons…"

Day three.

"Beat the yellowness from butter till peaking creamy white. To avoid curdling, slowly add brandy," I read, liberally spooning brandy as David whisked clouds of icing sugar from the butter bowl. "A splash of sherry enhances flavor…" The more we splashed, and taste-tested, the more we giggled. By then everything seemed funny.

Day four.

Walked country lanes sniping red berry sprigs of prickly holly from the hedgerow and snipped a bunch of mistletoe from a hollow oak in the field beside our cottage. Standing beneath it in the hall we kissed.

"Traditional." David smiled. Being newly-wed, we jumped at every excuse.

Day five.

Decorate. After assembling a wreath for our front door with a wire coat hanger, ribbon, paper flowers and ivy, we balanced holly sprigs over every picture frame downstairs.

Day six.

Huddled by the fire all day, peeled sweet chestnuts tossing skins to the flames. That done we pared the outer leaves from the Brussel sprouts. "Cutting crosses into each stem ensures even cooking." Checked the ingredients spread on the kitchen table— sausage-meat stuffing in breast, sage and onion the other end, bird trussed ready for next day.

Day seven.

Roast Bird. Steam pudding three hours. Decorate and set table.

Five hours later, David pulled the cooked bird from the oven.

"What the hell?" We stared horrified. Though nicely browned, the bird appeared standing upright on its stump legs. Its wings gruesomely outstretched.

"Oh. Oh, it's the damn tendons," we burst out laughing. "They must have contracted as they cooked. Now I see why Mrs. B said to pull them out."

Candles flickered. A cork popped. My beloved carved. The feast began.

Cheeks glowing, stuffed as the turkey we devoured, "Cheers," we toasted. "Merry English Christmas. Happy American Thanksgiving."

My mother died that next summer. Her life carried away with the setting sun. I love you, she whispered. I love you too, I croaked, casting her ashes to the autumn crocus and mountain iris of Hamilton Mesa where she loved to hike.

LINDA'S BOY

Still warm, the doe's legs and hooves stretched pointing toward the road. Head twisted, eyes glistening, open-—sighted on the green hillside across the highway she'd so nearly reached before the four-wheeled metal whirlwind struck.

The boy peddling his bike from school seeing death for the first time stopped, curious. His chance to find the life that had so recently sparked within her.

Dismounting, Linda's Boy unsheathed his knife, and guided by a Youtube demo on the laptop from his backpack, pierced the flesh below the doe's chin. Ran the bloody blade full length along her underbelly.

Inside the doe's womb the boy found, not the life source he sought but the still form of a perfect fawn. Cord severed, Linda's Boy bent his head to its nostrils. The first breath never came. He dug a hole. Obliterated death with a covering of earth weighted by a stone.

Carefully separating translucent fascia from flesh, he held it to the light and saw sky but not the freedom the doe sought. Folding the doe's soft hide, the boy carried it home. Pegged it on the ground to dry.

".... to decorate my bedroom wall." Displaying it to his mother, he smiled.

Not half a year passed when his mother, Linda, slipped from her body taking with her the life's seed he so sought. Remembering the ten years they'd shared so intensely, the boy sobbed, placed two lighted candles either side of her head, and shouted fro her to wake up. Not yet cold, not moving, eyes still shining, his mother, Linda stared, not at him, but far overhead at a place inside the flames' shadow steady on the ceiling.

Linda's boy took out his knife, sprang the blade. Scraped the cancer from her flesh, emptied her carcass with his hands and washing away the blood, sprinkled red pomegranate seeds gathered from his mother's garden.

He crawled inside her belly…the space where once he'd lain before his birth. Knees curled towards his chest, blanketing her parchment skin about him, Linda's Boy closed his eyes. Thumb to mouth, he held his breath. Waited. Waited to discover life.

Suddenly with no mother to care for, spur-of-the-moment, David and I hopped on a plane to see my two sons in London. Booked at the last minute, during the first leg, the short flight to Seattle, our seats were far apart. His, an aisle and mine, a middle.

I DON'T LIKE

Hi, she said squeezing into the middle seat between me and the African American, who studiously buried his nose in a book.

Pushing her carry-on under the seat in front of her, the young woman eyed us both deciding which of our ears to batter for the three-hour flight.

Not mine, I advertised lolled against the window, my eyes shuttered.

Gawd, am I tired. LIKE. I got up at three to make the airport on time. LIKE. So where did you come from then? Atlanta? LIKE. Via San Antonio, LIKE and now from Albuquerque. LIKE.

Her monologue began.

There must be a better way to Seattle. LIKE. Direct. LIKE, surely? So how long you in Seattle for. LIKE? Cos I was born and brought up there, LIKE. But I chose New Mexico see, to go to college. Now all my best friends are here. LIKE, so we get together to party once a year, LIKE. Ooo, so much white vodka last night you wouldn't believe. LIKE. My head should be splittin' but I'm used to that much liquor from my job in Seattle like. I'm a prison warden, like, though all the other girls with me are older—thirty-one, thirty-two. LIKE. See I'm only 29. LIKE. But I can hold my own. See, the Lock-ups mostly quiet except on Friday and Saturday nights. LIKE, when it's jam-packed with prostitutes all cussing, and angry. LIKE, screaming they shouldn't be there. LIKE. But one sign of trouble. LIKE, I tell them straight, "Ma'am. You need to step back inside your cell." One sight of my taser and they get the message. LIKE, and do as I say quiet as can be just as I told them. I may be small. LIKE, but I show them who's boss. LIKE, and tell them it won't go well when I take them up top next day and read my report to the Judge. LIKE. See it's my responsibility to get them ready for Court. LIKE. I do the paper work, cuff them an' take them up. LIKE. Meek as lambs they are next morning. Being a jailor is good. Shift work gives me time. LIKE, for my two girls. See it's just me and them, LIKE.

Her voice dropped, wistful, and I almost felt sorry for her.

But we jailor-moms stick together. LIKE, an' help one another out. You should see us weekends after work. LIKE. How we party. Kids in one room happy round the box with soda an' chips. LIKE. Us jailor moms downing white vodka till 2am. Zapping flies with our tasers and laughing. LIKE, 'bout some drunk we pulled over last week for DWI. LIKE, blubbing, 'Please, please, officer, just this once.' Thinks if he called me officer. LIKE, I'd let him go?' The nerve, LIKE. "No Sir, I told him straight. You're a danger to the community." LIKE, and I cuffed him and threw him in the slammer. LIKE.

Pausing, she snatched a breath.

Look there's Seattle. Now, to get to 176 to the motel where I'm staying. LIKE, I have to go north. LIKE, on 105. Then take 176 south in a couple of exits. LIKE. Lovely chatting with you folk. LIKE. Hasn't the time gone quick? LIKE.

Mmm. Uhhuh, her neighbor grunted closing his book.

Lucky for her, LIKE, she didn't hear my thinking.

LIKE. I muttered. *Go South, lady and all the way to hell, LIKE.*

*P*hew, thank goodness that's over, I sighed relaxing into our Business class seats for the long flight over the pond.

Munching salted pretzels over cocktails, David mentioned he'd liked to look up some long-lost friends he'd known in Malaysia. All he had was a postcard. Look, Nelson in Trafalgar Square. Here it is. I've kept it all this time. See the postmark. 1979. David turned over the picture to show the spidery message scrawled on the card's other side.

My new address is… the words read. "Cheers. Sam."

Sam became quite famous as a sort of Mr. Rogers of the East starring in a Singapore children's TV program. He dropped by most evenings after I moved into the flat across from his. Never known such a miserable man. Sailor Sam, his adoring fans called him. David paused.

We became friends. Really drinking buddies, I suppose. Need company? Brandishing a bottle of the local hooch and a pack of cards, he'd call already half way into my room."

Can't take another day. Seven years, I've survived that blasted kids' show, but enough is eee...nough. That's it. I've had it. Bugger it all. Damn people demanding autographs, pestering me with don't I know you from somewhere? As if we were fast friends. Sam would moan taking another swig.

Then one evening, the last time I saw Sam, he ranted on, almost crazed. WANTED, the next day his face plastered the headlines of every newspaper in Singapore. David twisted in his seat and stared. I never knew what happened to him after that. I can't believe the man's still alive and living in England's capital—not chained to the wall in some grim, Asian jail. Shaking his head as if hardly believing his own words, David began the story of Sailor Sam.

PAPER CASTLE

One afternoon, with no word to anyone, no hint to the TV Station, as his children's hour program came to an end, Sailor Sam looked directly into the eyes of his audience and announced,

"This is goodbye dear ones. You won't be seeing Sailor Sam again, my hearties. I bid you all farewell."

Waving a length of rope, he formed a loop, and dangled it swinging from his left hand out of camera range.

Expectant of a magic trick, the unseen children drew closer to their screens. Sam poked his head through the noose. Pulling the rope snug around his neck, he flopped his head to the left. Tongue lolling, eyes rolled into his head, he gurgled a series of choking, gasps. Then, to the horror of his young viewers and their parents, Sam ceased moving.

Too late, the producer yelled, Cut. Cut.

Sam vanished. Fled the country. The police never caught him.

After a couple of days of hard tourism in London, postcard in hand, David and I rode a number 9 bus to the grand deco building of the BBC, then began walking the nearby streets to locate the building where Sam had buried himself these past ten years.

Rounding a corner, we came upon a demolition sight of rubble and bricks of collapsed walls, but there in the destruction like an oasis in an inhospitable desert, stood one remaining building. Number 59. Its five stories barely intact. David ran his fingers down the faded list of long departed residents.

"Found him. He must still live here," David gasped in disbelief.

"Yes?" A voice crackled through the speaker in response when he pressed the doorbell.

"Sam. It's Dave, your friend from Singapore," David yelled.

Whispering, scrabbling followed.

"Can you come back in half an hour? We're not dressed."

My watch told 2pm.

The flats on the climb to the fifth-floor yawned empty, abandoned, their doors ajar. Broken glass littered, Sam's the only one still occupied.

"Come in. Come in. You're just in time." Sam peered from the narrow gap of an opened door revealing columns of newspapers stacked floor to ceiling along both walls. "Bastard landlord's hassling us to get us evicted. But our lease is good for six more months. And we're so comfortable here. Refuse to move. But welcome. Come in. Come in. I'll lead the way."

David and I glanced briefly at one another as we stepped inside.

"Act normal. Act normal." I commanded myself. "Don't on any account stare or show surprise."

Sam retreated backwards down the narrow passage remaining between the papers. Feeling my shoulders brush against the piles, I cautiously turned sideways for fear of knocking over a column. The door to the bathroom yawned open. Papers, newspapers in the tub. Newspapers along one wall, I controlled my gasp. Sam ushered us to the living room and indicated a niche containing two armchairs and a table constructed with woven strips of rolled newsprint.

"Here, make yourself comfortable," Sam invited removing an open Sunday Times from the table and blowing off the dust. "I'll go help Jenny with the tea. I'll be back in a jiffy."

"Sure. Take your time." I forced a relaxed smile, then made a face to David the minute he was gone, mouthing what the devil's going on?

I craned my neck seeking the world beyond the dust-streaked window frame. Normal. A waiting woman thrust out her arm. A red bus stopped in the street below allowing her to alight. All normal.

Thump, groan, a demolition ball collapsed the remaining wall of a neighboring building still partially standing rattled the walls around me causing a cloud dust to obliterate the outside, a world, which until that moment had been real. Cowering, I cast my eyes around the surreal scene. A claustrophobic panic gripped.

Had I fallen through a portal, rabbit hole or Alice's looking glass? Dismal black and white, the paper catacomb in which I sat replaced what once had been an elegant wall-papered drawing room. Dull with dust, glass drops of a multi-tiered chandelier trembled from a Georgian plaster ceiling rose. Bulging piles of more yet more newspapers indicated the contours of a once splendid mantelpiece on which no clock now stood or chimed.

My head swam as I sank into a wonderland of semi-consciousness and found myself sitting on the shoreline of a paper lake. Am I awake? Rivulets of pasted words and letters, both capital and lower case cascaded from the walls to form word-pools.

To orientate myself, I dipped in my hand and made a timid wave. The letter H and A surfaced.

"HA. HA." I whispered. "This is fun."

Then spotting the word SPLASH, I wet my face with the word WET, and waded into the lake up to my waist.

Half swooning, defying gravity, words flew from the walls, settling around me.

Loud honking in the street below brought me back.

"Hello. Hope I wasn't too long. We sleep during the day and work nights." Sailor Sam reappeared carrying a tray. Jenny behind him. The two of them perched on a low pile of newsprint in front of where we sat.

"Great to see you, man." They both grinned.

"Well what news?" Sam inquired, "We've a few minutes before Jenny and I need to get back to sleep. So much reading to do—can't ever seem to catch up," he waved his arm indicating the newspapers and words plastered on the walls.

The next ten minutes passed awkwardly.

"We work all night, see. She paints and I hang her paintings up on a line to dry as she finishes them." Sam stood up and shooed us out.

Not quite believing what we'd just witnessed, it took me a minute to adjust to the outside world. Traffic roared, pedestrians strolled the pavements, the buses ran. All looked normal. A rumbling roar made me look back. I could have sworn newspaper clouds filled the sky. No 59 disappeared.

An official letter from my London lawyers informing me my divorce case would be heard next summer, meant flying over the pond to England yet again. Finally, I exclaimed to a girl-friend, I can sever all ties from the bullying bastard I'd been shackled to for fourteen turbulent years. Whatever induced you marry such a guy? A friend questioned but I had no answer.

MARRY IN HASTE

"How about getting hitched? Today." My boyfriend Ed at the time shook me awake. "Cousin Jimmy says we can cross the border into Mexico and do the deed all in a day."

He'd laughed. Shoved his hands down my nightie. Roughly pinched his physical hold over me. Seven years. Jealous rages. Sobbed apologies quickly broken. Sweet forgivings. Pulverized, I'd shift-shaped. Vapid. Unrecognizable as me.

We were visiting his never-before-seen Mexican American cousin, Jimmy, whose father, now deceased, had forever abandoned 'Blighty,' (as we English fondly refer to England,) a generation back, struck a motherlode south of the Rio Grande, and taken up with a Mexican Beauty. "Gold? ...that's ours now." And the Mexican Government chased Jimmy's dad back across the border at gunpoint with only his skin. Jimmy's jet-black hair and fluent Spanish displayed his mix. He'd kept silent at school. 'Buenos dias' cost stinging slaps across his cheek. "Speak English, brat!" Now at fifty. Successful. Proud of the 'Li'l Red trucks' he sold. "Bisbee's premier dealership." He'd smiled. Coyly acknowledged his part ownership of a border Spanish-style motel where illicit transactions occurred.

Five days with Jimmy popped me outside my English box. Foreign. Everything. Arizona desert cactus, enchiladas, Jimmy's string of feeble jokes, elegant tea served by mini-skirted 'maids' at the Victorian Copper Queen Hotel, a recently revamped brothel; men decked out in jewels; spurred high-heeled boots and cowboy hats; couples two-stepping, clockwise in a Western Bar; Dos

XXs; the weight of light-free darkness two miles deep in Bisbee's Copper mine; 'rattlers,' a Circle K. selling Coke; and Jimmy's friend ranting how his grossly overweight son broke the seat when he'd illegally borrowed his Jaguar. "…while making-out…" he'd said, half proud. My ears flared red. *Was I hearing right?*

I sat up. Fully awake.

"Okay!" I answered, quickly weighing the odds, *If I marry it won't be legit back home. At the very least the bastard's finally showing a commitment. Might be a fun outing.*

I had a half decent skirt and matching top I'd bought for five bob at our annual village 'Jumblesale.' Read half a dollar for five bob; rummage sale for jumble. Jimmy picked up his girlfriend. Brass-haired, red splashed lips, softhearted, smiling, she pinned four corsages to our chests.

"Carnations? Orchids? A rose?" Whiteout mind. I have no recollection which.

Jimmy parked 'lil' red truck at the border fifteen miles south and we walked across. Jimmy slipped a $20 bill beneath the guard's typewriter.

'ADVOCATE.' The sign read above a doorway on Naco's single street. We were expected thanks to Jimmy.

"Bienvenidos." The 'Advocate's' daughter signaled 'follow.'

We passed two men sprawled over a counter. Curious. "Marriage witnesses," she inclined her head in explanation.

"$20 each." Jimmy paid.

In the back room, a man, complete with a bandit's handlebar mustache of movie-star proportions, and sporting a silver dollar sized turquoise and silver 'bolo' in lieu of a necktie, lifted his ten-gallon hat revealing black hair slicked flat.

"Bienvenidos. Welcome a Mexico y a mi pueblo." The Advocate beamed. Exchanged firm handshakes.

We flopped, sweat dripping. A desk fan stirred the air beyond our reach lifting the corners of the forms he spread across his desk.

"Full names; Bride's… Groom's… father, mother… Place of birth and d.o.bs.…" The form, endless. The pauses, eternal. He looked up. "Occupation: Groom's?"

"Lecturer in Modern German Fiction."

The Advocate leaped to his feet. Saluted crisply. "It is a great honor for me and for the town of Naco to marry a pro-fess-orr.…" He clasped my husband-to-be with a vice-grip handshake. He sat.

"Bride's father?"

"British Army Officer. 3rd. Gurkha Regiment. India…….."

Impressed, it seemed, by each profession up he jumped each time. Flourished a salute. "It is a great honor for me and for Naco to marry the daughter of a Col-on-nel." He sat.

And so it continued, "It is a great honor for me and for Naco to marry… the son of…, the daughter of …"

"Mother? Umm… housewife," I replied. Disappointed, he moved on.

"Bride's occupation?" He inquired.

"Speech Pathologist." I earned a handshake.

Yo-yos, we upped and downed, chair to standing, salute to proffered hand, smile to penetrating gaze. My smiling expression slipped from that expected of a bride.

Promises made, the ceremony over, Jimmy held out his hand.

"Marriage certificate?"

The Advocate held out his hand for Jimmy's cash. "First, doctor certificate so daughter copy in ledger." We turned, watched an exquisite script flow from her ink-pen.

The doctor's office should have been the last door on the left at the top of the street, upper corner where the hardtop ended and the dust road began, from the description we'd been given.

Arm-in-arm and overdressed we teetered the length of the single street. A group of men in striped prisoners-suits crowding an iron-barred window gawped, mouths open, as we past them, not once, not twice, but three times on our search. Up. Down. Up. Down and once again we repeated the exhibition to the prisoners' increasing astonishment.

"Yes. Yes, you were there." The Advocate redirected us back the way we'd come jabbing repeatedly.

The third trip we located the doctor in his dusty office behind a door we'd twice rejected.

"What him…the doctor?"

One of the previously lounging marriage-witnesses now sat posed behind a wooden desk. An antique blood-pressure gauge displayed his profession. Bare boards, two upright chairs, a fly-spotted calendar depicting a faded image of Guadalupe, the Madonna's hands extended in blessing. The room drooped, tired.

"You." He called my husband. Indicated I was to stay put.

Three questions the doctor asked. Was his bride under the age of sixteen? Sane? Suffering from syphilis?

"Non, non, and non," my partner answered in Spanish, at which the doctor extended his palm. "…for certificate…" Jimmy handed over a twenty.

At the office, the Advocate's daughter still scribed, pen dipping, painstaking intent. *"Lonche. Dos horas. Pronto."* She tapped her wrist. Mimicked chewing.

In the local bar across the road and facing the border, stemmed, salt-rimmed plastic glasses brimming countless margaritas were raised and downed.

"To Mexican marriage! To the bride and groom! To lovers everywhere! To us! To Jimmy who made it all possible! To the power of the dollar bill!"

"Wife. Husband." The two words tasted sour on my tongue

when I got back to England. "Oh well, a Mexican marriage is hardly binding." I consoled myself. "Stubbs! … Mrs.-worn-down-pencil… Mrs.-stubbed-cigarette-butt." I shivered and vowed to never use his ugly name.

"You did what? You married where…?" My friends asked aghast, when I announced the deed back in England. "Naco! Mexico! Seriously?"

"Its not legal," I reassured.

Wrong, wrong, wrong.

"If the marriage is deemed legal in the country of origin, it's deemed legal in Britain," lawyers informed.

Two long years of wrangling, it took to un-hitch. To unearth the original hand-written entry in the Advocate's ledger, long buried beneath a paper mountain.

Jimmy knew a man, who knew the man with whom to place a fistful of greenbacks. But for him we could never have unmarried.

Marry in Mexico, repent at leisure.

Yep, I learned the truth of that statement.

Cut loose from marriage, I changed my name legally, and reverting to my maiden name, pondered what lay ahead. Clearly continuing to cut and fold 9-gauge steel in the elements was out after a road accident forced me to give up working outdoors cutting eight-foot sheets of steel to take up something gentler. But what?

"Sit on your hands and do nothing to create a vacuum for your passion to reveal itself. Commanded the book I was reading. So, I sat. I sat and I sat kicking my proverbial heels. I waited for the vacuum to fill.

Over a year later, a long-forgotten encounter with a fortune-teller came to mind. I see writer, I recalled her telling me back then. Hmm, now there's an idea, I thought. Might as well pick up my pen and join the South West Writers group and learn the dos and don'ts of writing craft.

SHE SAW IT IN HER CRYSTAL BALL

"I can't help it. I see writer."

"No! You've got it wrong." I argued. "I am an artist, a painter, a sculptor."

The Gypsy Fortuneteller raised her eyes and looked up sharply from her crystal ball, stared, and shrugged.

"You will write. That is how you'll make your name. Late in life." The reading clearly over, I passed a silver coin over her open palm as custom required.

I was twenty, sitting in a tented booth at an English country village fete. The gypsy tugged her paisley headscarf, and tossed her head, jangling gold hoop earrings.

After I left school, I did as all good girls should, chose a career to benefit mankind. "Art is nothing more than a selfish hobby." The school Principle glared, stressing Selfish. Obediently, I forgot about art as a career. I became a Speech Therapist. Helped old men and women communicate again, after they'd been struck speechless by a stroke, and helped young children unscramble the sounds we human beings use to label objects, actions and our thoughts. I gave them tools to articulate their needs through speech or play. Sometimes I worked to free adults trapped developmentally in a two or four year old's child's world. They loved me, and I them, neither one of us any worse, nor better, than the other.

I ached to be first in someone's life. Anybody's life. I married. I bore two sons. I traveled. Australia, Bahrain, Muscat,

Cyprus. A Royal Naval Officer's wife, trapped in twin-sets and pearls, and too many official parties drinking horse's necks, chattering nonsensical small talk, I shriveled inside. Painting saved me. Riding sidesaddle behind my friend Jos, we 'scooted' on her Vesper, sketching Bahrain's date-palm groves, dhows, Mosques, and hidden courtyards. From the rooftop, a blind man carrying a lidless kettle, stumbled across the wasteland that surrounded my house, led by a child holding his stick horizontally, unaware we watched him squatting to relieve himself, or that we sketched his private moment, as he cleansed between his thighs, pouring water in a thin trickle from the kettle. Another day, resplendent in his orange turban, Jos and I beguiled a Baluchi Tribesman to pose for us, though his religion forbade depiction of 'God's likeness'. Long forgotten, God's likeness now lies in my son's attic on its side.

Posted on exchange with the Aussie Navy, my husband sailed East for nine long months out of twelve. Pregnant, bored and lonely, I enrolled in a workshop. "A mistake" I decided, during the very first class. "Barking crazy fool." I ignorantly judged my teacher. Our assignment, take a handful of clay. Create nineteen models to illustrate… She listed abstract ideas. Tension. Space. Volume. Intervals. Unity. Light…I read from the orange notebook, I kept, a reminder of my arrogance. "These add up to a total sculpture." She concluded. I smirked. Space? Intervals? Attention? I stayed because I had paid the full semester. Quickly, I understood who was the fool. Me. Ignoramus. I still have the negative of my sculpture, the holes I carved now solid. Space does have shape I discovered.

In Sydney, embarrassed by my hobby, my husband threw my sculptures into the weeds, over our passion fruit hedge at the bottom of our garden. I decided. Divorce. If I was to live, our marriage must die. Simple.

Except it wasn't simple. We made our two boys fatherless by that act. We returned to separate homes in England. Overnight, I became a single mother, struggling with two children. Each day we walked along Portsmouth's seafront, and played a while, digging holes into the English cold pebble beach. I was my eldest son's lifeline to the hearing world. By an ironic twist of fate, he was born profoundly deaf. "No useful hearing" He was diagnosed. "He must attend a school for the deaf." A tiger protecting her young, I snarled. "But no-one can speak there. How do you expect him to learn?"

I became my son's speech therapist, his teacher. I panicked if a day passed without my cramming him with one new idea or word. I knew the learning curve slowed at five, that time was short. Then, when he was seven, his teacher gently told me. "He has language. Your job is done, now. Relax. Be his mother." And my sons and I cuddled close, looked at picture books, and laughed playing hide-and-seek in the bracken of Richmond Park.

My boys, both grown, now attended college. I packed up and moved to America.

I was free.

Little point changing just location, everything had to change. I was adamant. I tore up my diploma. "I am a sculptor." I practiced my response to the question, what do you do?

"Two dimensional, her works are primary colored, cut and folded steel," my resume declared. Joyous figures, they made many people smile. Non-verbal communication, verbal communication, not so different to Speech Therapy after all.

Santa Fe, New Mexico, art capital of the world. Late 80s. The timing was perfect. "Decide. Are you a floor or wall person?" A Canyon Road Gallery insisted, handing me my first check. I joined the Artists Co-op, downtown. My work sold. Investing in a plasma cutter, I taught myself to cut 9-gauge steel, often searing holes through my heavy boots and green suede apron, fashioned from a thrift-store skirt.

"Am I mad?" I asked myself, ten years later. "Here I am in goggles, helmet, noise, dust and freezing cold, risking slicing off my hands, while my friends work calmly in warm studios listening to Bach. I must change direction.

Two years and three months, was the time it took. I fretted, sitting for never-ending hours on my hands waiting for the vacuum to fill. Impatient, I flew to San Miguel Allende for six weeks, and bought a bag of clay. Clay, wet and soft, my hands laid seven egg-shaped heads, explored their three dimensions. My Santa Fe studio filled with the sweet notes of North Indian chants, peaceful, content. Pounded flat, and danced on with my feet, I rolled, paddled and scraped. Boulder-heads, minimal, primitive, stared unblinking. Figures, beaten from whole bags of 'supersculpt', then cast in bronze, stood sentinel. The yard, the studio overflowed. Galleries across the States showed my work. "A second-runger." Content, I recognized which rung I stood upon. I could not schmooze. I could not sell. I could not climb the ladder to the top.

I married my David after eighteen years. "Be nice to my English friend." Romona threatened, introducing us to one another from the flatbed of her truck, at the Galisteo Village Rodeo.

And he was, though he joked he didn't know what the hurry was.

Last year, I scraped my final bag of clay empty. Joyless, lifeless objects, every one, I dumped them into the arroyo. Pulling the plug from my kiln, I removed it to Craig's List.

I picked up the pen.

With the ghost of the gypsy fortune teller peering over my shoulder, I began to type.

"For my father and all those desert frogs waiting for the rains to sing." Reads the dedication page of POET UNDER A SOLDIER'S HAT, the book I penned in my father's voice. I see now, I should also have included my name, for like my father, I too carry the label late developer. Making up for forty lost years, words, stream onto paper, seeking voice.

If he had never buried his talent by joining the army...If I had not been such a goody-good girl back in my twenties... England floated far behind me as at last I headed for the open road.

I'd taken a step, emerged from the void and discovered I could write. Nowadays, without my asking, words happen in my head. Sometimes dreaming paragraphs, my fingers groping for the computer keys, tap Undo. Redo. Backspace. Delete, while I sleep.

"Late in life. I see writer." Perhaps the gypsy foretold my future right

POET UNDER A SOLDIER'S HAT

Caught in two World Wars, pre-Mutiny skirmishes, and the Great Sepoy Rebellion, the true saga of lives not so "pukkha" as might be supposed. My father Hugh's back-story exposes child marriage, an adulterous a air over many summers in a Himalayan Hill Station, illegitimate pregnancies and banishment to England. More a poet than a soldier, Hugh, a British Officer of the Raj, serves with the 3rd Queen Alexandra's Own Gurkha Rifles in the Kyber Pass bordering the Northwest Frontier Afghanistan. Mountain trekking, skiing, gentlemen's sports, bandits, tribal warlords, missionaries, ordinary men and ghosts are not enough.

Bored, Hugh seconded to the Political and Foreign Service in Arabia, Persia, and Waziristan, until disgraced, he is "invited" to return to his regiment. A naked Colonel's dictum "conformity kills" guides Hugh's adventurous life. Partition frees both India and Hugh.

Maybe mine as well.

THE END. I typed on the final page.

Step one, my first book over and done. An unknown, with a self-published book, by E.P.Rose, my name jumped from the Amazon page. I read the reviews. Wow. Really, I'd written that book. But to declare, Author? Writer? Neither description sat right, so if anyone wanted to know what I did, I've just finished my first book, I'd reply.

My computer suddenly silent and my days empty, David and I fled south. A month in a Mexican hut made entirely of bamboo on a jungle hillside overlooking Playa La Ropa's bay sounded the stuff of dreams.

Ninety-nine. Hurrah, we'd exclaim each time summiting the final stone slab. 99 steps from the beach to our Palapa eyrie high in the leafy canopy. From our hammocks sudden sparks of light flashing between the leaves reached me from the sea.

As a change from my usual shut-eyed, cross-legged meditation, I decided to compose one children's poem every morning. One month later, my notebook overflowed with loosely written verse and drawings, enough to create a book for children of any age. Words could be fun and set a child's mind spinning. What, for example, could a child imagine hearing a Pipol Tree grew in a country called India?

DITTY DOTTY DITTIES

This collection of verse opens up a world of language delightful to children of all ages and those who read to them. Elizabeth penned these poems and drawings daily as dawn broke over the Mexican beach.

PIPOL TREE
in India they have a pipol tree
it must be the strangest of sights to see
is it a bit like a person sort of leafy and tall
or a bit like a strong man lifting them all

EL ARBOL PIPOL
el árbol Pipol de la India
cosa mas rara que verse puedan
un poco como una persona tipo frondosa y alta
o un poco como un hombre fuerte que a todas alza

FOOTPRINTS
following footprints in the sand
I wonder whom I walk behind
some prints are so wide with toes so long
some very faint and others strong
jumping great steps to match their stride
I try to fit mine right inside
turtles leave tracks
you do too
do you know which ones belong to you

HUELLAS
sigo huellas en la arena
me pregunto detrás de quién camino
algunas anchas con dedo finos
algunas muy tenues y otras muy marcadas
doy grandes pasos para coincidir con sus zancadas
intento calzar mis pies dentro de ellas
tortugas hacen huellas
también las haces tú
sabes cuales te pertenecen a tí

For twelve years now, we've met. My poet/painter girlfriend and I. Two hours. Sunday mornings. We get together to sometimes praise, but more often critique one another's prose. WAS. WENT. THAT. LIKE … Boring, boring we'd say. SHOW not TELL. A Master Class on the craft of writing, we called our weekly sessions. No point being always being nice-nice, we agree. Without her input my writing would have long ago died. Thanks to my friend's prodding, I've five books to my name, one a chap book of poetry.

I looked around for someone to record my PUSH book on tape. Has to speak old fashioned pukka English to match my father's voice. But where to find such a person in New Mexico.? Why, Santa Fe of course.

We know someone, mutual friends declared. And so it was we met Hugh, an Englishman who read THE TIMES, spoke with a perfect upper-class accent and had even briefly worked in India with the BBC.

How do you do, he introduced himself over a cup of coffee. And when he spoke, I heard my father. You even share my father's name, I told him, Hugh.

Hugh stood no taller than my chest. Reaching for my hat and scarf from the coffee shop's coat rack as we left the café, I got to wondering about his life. How my life would be if I... My mind drifted... a story manifested from the ether.

GEORGE THE BLACKSMITH

George selected a 5lb hammer. A nail held firmly across the flatbed of the anvil between thumb and forefinger. His right hand swung up and down. With one strike the angled nail flattened straight. Another wham spread the metal toothpick-thin. He held it up to the grimed windowpane checking, dropped it point first into an empty coffee tin with a sigh.

George the Blacksmith, just George to his family, butt of nobody's cruel name-calling, his dingy forge was where he felt the happiest.

A shadowy figure in the light filtering through a veil of cobwebs over the small window, he grabbed a handful of misshapen nails from the spiky mound beside him on the dirt floor, selected five and held them pressed between his lips. One by one hammered each to a blade. For an hour he worked, back curved, head down, sleeves rolled, hairy forearms bulging, lifting, dust-grimed hands obedient to his mind. The misshapen nails were all that remained of his life as a farrier.

He straightened, rubbing the small of his back. The hump on his right shoulder, now apparent, bowed his body to a stoop shifting his leather apron lopsided. Right side higher than the left. Grasping the coffee tin with both hands, he shook it, nodded...the clunk of nails settling, the weight of it... Faint movement of his lips hinted a smile. Row nine. Fifty-six from the left. June 11. He stacked the coffee tin on the shelf, tucked the date inside his head.

"Enough for today,George, my man," he told himself. Okay.

Okay. Who cares if flattening nails is a little weird. It harmed no one. Part of him recognized his obsession. Seeing his wife's sour face in his mind, he pushed back the cloud of self-doubt. Stepped from the shed into the light. Yes, blacksmithing gave his life purpose.

"Well?" Sarcastic, his wife Lilly demanded when arriving home, and he flopped into his favorite chair beside the hearth. "So how many useless nails today?"

"For the want of a nail. A shoe was lost. For the want of a shoe…dah-dah, a horse…" George snarked, "Don't fret, woman. You'll see when the time comes. I have plans." His stock answer did nothing to mollify his wife's persistent questioning. Only served to reinforce his determination He smirked to show he held a precious secret. "One day lassie…." was all he's say in answer to his wife's sneer.

Most afternoons, his work in the smithy finished, weather permitting, George took Strawberry for a run to the moors. A Clyde roan, his horse towered fifteen hands to his four feet. To mount Strawberry, George constructed a mount of seven steps. My "stairway to heaven, he liked to joke. In a way it was. Same as for any full-grown man, perched on Strawberry's broad back, the grass fields, yellow gorse, hedges and open moorland spread below unhindered.

George clambered onto the granite platform he'd built to reach her saddle and called, "Hup. Hup. Hup. Come now lassie."

Strawberry turned, pricking her ears, ambled slowly to where George waited with the saddle. Girth pulled tight, stirrup leathers adjusted, gripping the pommel George thrust his size two boot into the child-sized stirrup, and with a heave swung his free leg over the saddle. Deflating her belly with a tap of his boots Strawberry lifted her tail and fired a gun-rattle of air.

"…and a *tally-ho* to you, my fine, four-footed lady friend,"

As she exhaled George pulled her girth in a notch. Taking her reins, signaled her forwards and headed out.

Two miles down the lane, hearing Strawberry's clop approach, Critchley, George's nearest neighbor and only real friend, glanced up from his cabbage patch and paused leaning on his hoe. Long used to George's frog-like figure crouched knees to chest on the giant horse, Critchley no longer saw him as "that little humpback."

"Fine day for a ride, George," he greeted as always. "There's a pint fer yer on yer way home if you've a mind of stopping by."

For nine years they shared a drink together at least several times a week. A habit they'd developed after Critchley's wife was taken by the Spanish Flu'.

His mind set on the moor ahead, George looked over without reining in Strawberry and gave a nod. Fretful as greyhounds at the starting gate, the smell of the open moor in their nostrils, horse and man chomped to be beyond the confines of the matted bramble, blackthorn and hazel-hedged lane eager to let loose on firm peat land beyond the marsh. Trusting Strawberry's sure footing, he let Strawberry pick her way along a well beaten sheep run twisting between the treacherous mud pools that lurked beneath the too-bright green bog-marsh.

Safely across and on firm turf, Strawberry stretched her neck pulling the reins from George's control, and tail streaming broke from a trot into a full gallop on reaching the moor. No need directing her, she knew as well as George where they were headed.

George could not risk a fall. He would never be able to remount. He knew that. Wrapping the reins about his wrists, for the next twenty minutes, the only sounds were the soft thud of hooves striking sheep-cropped grass, the creak of leather, the pant of his and Strawberry's breath and the rush of air whistling in George's ears. A mother skylark's cry of alarm rose from her nest hidden in the purple heather startling them both.

Panting, Strawberry pulled back to a gentle plod allowing George to push himself upright. He raised his arms saluting the sky, the sun, scudding clouds, the lone oak tree growing near the brown waters of the Loch where they were headed. Scattering a flock of flat-tailed sheep, Strawberry halted beneath the lowest branch of the oak just long enough for George to reach up, wrap his fingers around the branch, and in one gymnastic swing mount the oak's broad limb.

From his eyrie he watched Strawberry wade into the shallow loch among the rushes following expanding circles rippling from her lips across the water as she drank.

George settled among the leaves, back against the trunk's rough bark, high above the ground, pinpoints of sunlight pulsating between the leaves. His thoughts erased, drifted weightless no longer earthbound, no longer a little man. Powerful, king of all he surveyed, he flushed with the certitude of his existence. An instantaneous feeling of wellbeing swept over him.

My Oak. I'm home, he murmured closing his eyes. The physical contact. The support of her sturdy trunk holding him, the broad limb he sat astride firm between his thighs. Back pressed to her body, he allowed his head to rest in the cleft of the splayed trunk behind him. Tree: man. Man: woman. No different from how he felt curled in his wife's lap, his head nuzzled to her bosom. He searched the years trying to recall their last touch of tongues, the surge of lust, the last time she stirred his groin. Rare, now they'd both reached middle age. No real loss. Not worth the grieving.

Dreaming nails, creating his *big surprise*, an hour zipped passed. Day began its downward slide behind Kestor's granite mass. A leaf brushed George's cheek. Its oak kiss. He shifted, opened his eyes, located Strawberry. Contentedly grazing, her dappled roan-pink coat, her white-feathered hocks pretty against the green of the rough grass.

"Hup. Hup," George summoned. "Home girl."

Pricking her ears, she lifted her head and ambled over to still beneath the branch allowing George to drop back onto her back.

Ignoring George's sawing of her reins, Strawberry took the bit between her teeth and set off for home at a gallop. Oats waited. Time to be rid of the saddle burdening her back.

Nearing Critchley's, no need to call out, his friend stood in his doorway, pipe in mouth, his black lab, Ben, at his feet, waiting to steady George as he slipped to the ground.

"Come in. Come in," he greeted leading the way to his cottage.

"Get off with yer," Critchley exclaimed swiping his cat Blackie off the kitchen table where she slept curled up in a pool of sunlight. "Take a seat, George."

George felt right at home. The dust on the floor, ashes spilled from the wood range, the smell of tobacco from Critchley's pipe resting on a saucer, a mug of tea-dregs cold since breakfast.

That man lives like an animal, Lilly would sniff whenever she visited, which wasn't often. Yer, more comfortably than me, George would retorted silently.

"See what yer think of this 'un," said Critchley handing George a foaming tankard of his latest home brew.

Matching sip for sip, George and Critchley downed their beer signaling their approval with nods, terse phrases and an occasional burp.

"Good head on it,"

"Err, a strong 'un, this."

Weather and health aside not much other chat passed between them. Patting his belly, George wiped a hand across his mouth signaling the session's end.

"Best be gettin' home before dinner's set."

"Give yer a leg up then?"

Interlacing fingers fashioning a step, Critchley braced firm while George clambered onto Strawberry. George leaned down and shook Critchley's hand.

"Thanks pal. Good seein' yer." He said taking up Strawberry's reins, and with a gentle *Hup Hup* headed for home.

Week in week out, for years the same routine. Then one day….

Returning from the hutch across the yard one afternoon, a "dispatched" rabbit dangling lifeless from his hand, George sniffed, already tasting the stew his wife promised. Knowing better than to truck muck-plastered gumboots into the kitchen, "I'll skin and gut the rabbit out here," he called from outside. Receiving no answer he leaned his head round the door.

Eyes to the ceiling his wife lay on the flagstone floor, a partially peeled onion resting on her open palm, a paring knife at her fingertips. Never again to call him her man, never again to cuss him. With never a goodbye between them, his beloved was gone. Critchley and he buried her on the knoll behind his house.

Silent forever, cornflowers clutched against her heart, she rested to one side of the same knoll chosen for his creation.

Weeks passed. Rarely rising from his kitchen chair, head dropped forward, back rounded as his hump, and hands limp on his lap, George sat un-seeing while congealed food-scraps, unwashed plates and half drunk cups of tea strewed the table. It was a sunbeam through the windowpane one afternoon that caught his eye. George looked up. Five weeks of grieving over.

"Tomorrow at sparrow-fart, I'll start on the nails," George spoke aloud. Nail by nail he'd placed them, every one, those many nights when sleep eluded him. Clear as an architect's blueprint. So clear in fact his project already bore a name. "Walking Giant with Snake Stick."

The making of it filled his days with purpose. Nail by nail, soldered, welded, beaten, the 8-foot effigy gestated atop the hillock sheltering the smithy. George dug and filled five holes. Boulders and cement for footing, a dozen re-bars embedded for an armature, from bare skeleton to ironclad, each nail cross-hatched, covering the form—all but its head-space, eyes, nostrils, parted lips—those he sketched in outline only. Grey, blue, cloud, sun, moon and stars reflected man and sky's ever-changing moods. Through two drilled piercings, his snake-stick kept watch. Keeping his sleeping wife abreast of progress George chattered on aloud.

Nine full months and it was done. The giant strode tall, arms swinging, snake walking stick in hand—a beacon to the surrounding hamlets, an icon to all.

All of a sudden a celebrity, locals in pubs and markets pointed, "That's him. George, the man who made the Giant up there on the hill."

He was a man. He knew it. Walking home across the snow one afternoon, his back against the setting sun, before him stretched his shadow larger than life, full grown, a giant of a man—long-legged, full-bodied, stepping free.

Poets are supposed to have a chapbook and the reading is in just ten days.

Help, I called my computer friend, the friend who designed and formatted all my writing.

Heads together, in two days the manuscript headed to the printers. Eight days to have the printed copies in my hand to present at the group reading in Albuquerque. A miracle for sure...thought to finish, ten days in all. I waved a chapbook.

PORTRAITS

digging

what are you doing? I asked
I am digging for my roots she answered
puzzled *will you find them buried?* I persisted
of course she nodded *they're holding up this tree*
and pointed where the beech tree's silver trunk
exploded green into blue

that's my home
that's me
I am the tree

she put down her spade
sat beside me
pressed my hand against the bark
feel she insisted *I am alive*

and handed me her spade
now you dig she encouraged
turning I found myself alone

listening for your return

seeking you
each morning   ear pressed against your door
straining for the slow shuffle-scrape
your slippers etch   across the flagstone floor
fearing   a hollow echo   I hesitate
before
letting drop   the brass knocker
we chose together
before
without a word   you vanished   that
thursday evening two long months ago
cobwebs bind shut the windows
shield the yellowed tablecloth
our two places   expectant
on the kitchen table
no aromatic vapor
escapes the iron casserole
its half-moon handle   smooth from years of lifting
hangs cold   lifeless   on the hob
each visit   the cottage sinks   and
I must bend lower to part its ivy tendrils
did a blackberry vine tumble you into the river
sweep you downstream   face   turned hawk-ward
to the gold hidden in the sun
come my love
I obey your whisper
rest my axe against the wall   stack pinon
newly cut
in the willow basket
I wove for you last winter

Will you marry me? David proposed for the second time taking my hand one morning during breakfast. Sorry but I'm not getting down on my knees, he said.

Two years had passed since the first time he'd pulled me close while we were hiking in the woods above our friends' cabin in Chromo, Colorado. I want to spend my life with you he said.

I made room in my closet for his clothes, replaced my coffee table for his.

When David moved down from his house on the hill into mine. Happy days sipping wine together in the back yard under the pink-petal rain of the peach tree.

I don't know what the hurry is, he joked when we were legally hitched in Santa's Fe's courthouse. We've only being going out only eighteen years. We laughed, toasted one another with salt-rimmed margarita and flew to Sri Lanka.

Two, three years slipped by.

Back in New Mexico, Summer blazed particularly hot and dry. Scorched grass and parched scrub. No sign of green anywhere but on acres of water-guzzling golf courses. New Mexico prayed for an early monsoon to quench the thirsty earth with the expected annual heavy rains. Wild fires raged. Tempers frayed, and I, and all my friends, fidgeted on edge, waiting for the rains that never came.

APPREHENSION

Nothing tangible, nothing unusual, but all that one August day, through the house the woman padded—front door to kitchen door, bare-footed, looking, listening. *Something just doesn't feel right,* she muttered opening, checking, then closing the back door for the umpteenth time.

South across the basin, ten-miles of shimmering high desert grassland, disembodied pinon, cedar, cholla, leached pale by summer, stretched unchanged.

She scanned the thousand-foot cliff-line ten miles south of her house where sky and earth connected. And, which until that year, had flowed east to west unspoiled by human hand.

Now a rectangular eruption of a New Yorker's ugly, weekend folly gouged nature's linear skyline.

The woman sniffed. Intent. Head tilted. Peered for some invisible difference she was unable to identify. A flock of starlings looped loops overhead, their squawks shattering the silence.

"Daft fool." The woman scolded herself aloud. "Go back indoors and calm down."

A little comforted by the sound of her own voice, obeying herself, she did. But once inside, she resumed her to-ing and fro-ing—kitchen, living room, back, front. Pad. Pad.

Snapping the Yale catch, she flung the front door wide surprising her neighbor's yellow dog crouched mid-poop on her patch of dirt, inside her front gate.

"GRRRRRR-off with you. WhaaHHH!" The woman flapped her arms. "Not in my yard, you don't. Bugger off filthy cur," she shouted.

Shamed, the yellow beast slunk off. Tail up, stiff legged, to hunker down again where the road beyond her yard wound towards the village.

Standing in the doorway, sunlight beamed red through her eyelids. Her nostrils flared, inhaled heat. The draft's ruffling chill tunneling from the back door, delightful on her spine, she smiled,

Back inside, mid morning, blinds pulled shut against the sun, the woman flopped legs sprawled, flipped the on switch. Surfed the TV's mid-morning channels. Last week's catastrophe forgotten, no beeps, no disaster warnings flashed. No collapsed buildings, flooded homes, and tear-streaked faces, thankfully those last week's upsetting images were gone. Wiped from the screen. But not her mind. The woman saw them still—toddlers, wide-eyed, adults' stuffing crumpled photographs inside ragged shirts still scrabbling the rubble seeking mementos of their past.

"Which treasures would I most mourn if I were dispossessed?" She mused to herself. "What keepsake would I grab? For sure that family snapshot taken by a stranger at the seaside …husband, children and me captured, smiling. Passports, credit cards… Yes, those I'd snatch." Drowsy, an hour passed.

Chuff-chuff-chufffffff.

What the hell….? Strange noises arrested her reverie. Came closer. A steam-engine? Breath suspended, her neck hairs alarmed. She forced herself to creep from the living room towards the sound.

"Lord-save-us, Tammy. You'll give me a heart attack. How the devil did you get in?" She let go her breath. Let her chest deflate.

Puff-puffing, relentless on her mission, Tammy-tortoise never paused. Tammy-tortoise dragged slowly up the corridor towards her away from the back door.

The children discovered her munching on a rose two years before. Please. Please can we keep it? They'd begged till she relented. And so it was Tammy stayed, became the family's pampered pet plumping up on cabbage leaves and strawberries.

As the woman bent to throw Tammy-tortoise out, Tammy yawned, drooling, showed the pinkness of her gums. Unstoppable, Tammy clambered the woman's toes and heaved onto the hump of her left foot, and promptly laid an egg. Soft-shelled. Squelchy.

"Oooophff. Revolting creature. Out." The woman shuddered. No midwife, her, gingerly holding Tammy's shell, kicking open the door, the woman deposited Tammy-tortoise in the back yard.

A breeze blew strong. She smelled smoke. The horizon had disappeared, swallowed by a grey-black cloud. She saw flickering orange tongue rise from the New Yorker's roof on the distant ridge and flames of red streak into the basin.

The woman slammed shut the door. Ran the corridor. Flinging open the front door she glimpsed a string of fire-trucks scream the road. Then she heard them. Sirens.

A police car cruised. "Mandatory evacuation. Twenty minutes to collect your things."

Panting, she ran inside. "Passports, credit cards… what else, what else?"

The image of the shell-less egg Tammy tortoise laid on my foot wouldn't leave, nor the sense of foreboding troubling me. An omen? Was Tammy alerting me? To what I puzzled?

But something was awry. David's left arm no longer swung in step as he walked. He had a hard time bending the fingers of one hand. He stumbled on the cobbled square in Venice. Couldn't see where to sign his name on the hotel registration form.

You have Parkinson's Disease, The Neurologist dumped the diagnosis in our laps, stabbed us in the heart.

I wasn't too surprised. Parkinson's The egg. The omen I feared. The omen Tammy had warned me about.

His symptoms controlled by medications, we pushed the evidence aside and carried on with our lives more or less as before. Golden years we called them, the decade after his diagnosis, the time when David could still drive, eat out in public and live life to the full. I remember us hiking into the desert silence of White Sands not wearing any clothes and gazing at the Milky Way wondering at our existence.

"Oh David, David," I whispered, clutching him one time in bed. "There's a mouse in the room. Listen."

We froze. There it came again scratch, scrabble, scratch. Faint. Persistent.

"It's me. My tremor. My toes. On the sheet."

Our lives would never be the same again.

SMALL PRINT

something was awry that morning

half-eaten tins   spilled tomato paste on every surface   littered
evidence of his unremembered midnight feasting

catch him before he slips away

fingers pressed lightly on his pulse   a wire coat hanger swung
from his arm
proud   look   he said…a new way to take blood pressure

rivers   peed yellow on my bedroom wall   woke me with its
streaming

deep down he must hate me

pointing at a grove of palms one holiday
he urged   look behind you…twelve people in dinner jackets
wearing ice skates on their heads

they must have gone now   I soothed

cross-legged quietly on my bed I shut my eyes   prayed
help   my sweet lover is drowning in his Parkinsonian sea

check his medication an unseen angel whispered

thank you   I took his hands   waited for a lucid moment to tell
my madman he was mad   pretend   you are a doctor   and
your patient is behaving oddly   I smiled
silent   he checked the phial's small print

    ....in some cases .... hallucinations may occur

taking one pill less each day   coconuts reappeared on palms   ice
skates melted

Though we tried there was no escape. A shadow, the Parkinson's thief was always with us. Sri Lanka, Ayurveda in Kerala, India... Mexico of course. We were always happy traveling.

How about Yelapa? No cars, no malls, the only way to get there is by boat, it's supposed to be a paradise.

Six weeks on the traffic-free peninsula in Palapa for rent. Six weeks living in a bamboo hut? Too tempting to ignore, we quickly pre-paid its rental. If it's too good to be true.... Too soon we learned the truth of that saying.

VOICE FROM THE GRAVE

Sometimes escape is impossible. For weeks it was Emerson this, Emerson that. On the radio, TV, every magazine I picked up. Beyond his fame, I knew nothing about the man. Even on the plane on my way to Mexico. Opening an old New Yorker there was his name again. Emerson...... I read every word and quote.

David and I sped far out across the bay, away from the tourist town of Puerto Vallarta to the isolated peninsular of Yelapa. A full month. No cars, no roads, the only transport mules, and our own two feet. Everything arrived by boat—cement, groceries, bricks, machines...

Off loaded onto Yelapa's small wooden jetty, two lads grabbed our bags.

"Where you go?" They exchanged looks and all but changed their minds when we told them. "Top of hill. Cost more. $5 a bag."

The boys headed up a steep jungle path into the trees. We followed panting. After fifteen-ish minutes, the boys plonked the cases and bag of snorkeling gear on the leaf mold.

"We no work for tacos," they leered folding their arms threateningly. "$10 extra or leave you here."

With nothing but thick bamboo and jungle in sight we agreed. Another twelve minutes scramble later, an even narrower uneven path over tree roots brought us to a wooden gate. Inside, a clearing revealed a tropical garden and a Palapa-style house draped with bougainvillea.

We'd booked the palapa on the Internet and stupid that we were, paid up front as demanded by the SF landlady. "Does it have easy access? My husband has a balance problem. Is it close to the sea?" I double checked. 'Yes. Yes.' She'd replied. The photo looked so lovely we'd paid up.

"You're up there," the landlady grunted pointing further up the garden hillside to a level area. "You'll find all you need," she lied.

The small circular Palapa could be reached only by negotiating a single stone bridge over a drainage canal. The sleeping loft was inaccessible to my husband. We settled on two outdoor beds instead. One, the widest and most comfortable in the tree canopy, and one, mine, isolated on the walkway against a fence tight to an abandoned cemetery.

"Now you stay over there on your own side." I firmly told the spirits of the dead as I settled for my first night. "No visiting allowed."

But they were there alongside me. Hovering. Spirits watched. Me naked under the outdoor shower, me in the cracked mirror as I brushed my teeth, and swung beside me in the hammock hung eye-level in the canopy. I burrowed beneath the flimsy sheet and bed cover and four beach towels I piled on top to keep the cemetery's inmates' icy breath from freezing me to death. To be sure they didn't touch me, I wound a towel round my head. The air howled cold.

No beach the next day, nor the following six. Holed up in our eerie the wind's moaning never ceased.

"Come, visit," the Spirits whispering insisted.

I found a gap in the fence-line beyond the shower stall, and scrambled through into the Graveyard.

Bedraggled weeds, fallen headstones greeted me. "Jose. Maria. Eduardo. Isabel…," I spoke their names then stopped.

"For our friend Emmy. 1952." A hand-painted cross in English proclaimed.

Poor abandoned soul, I mouthed tugging at the vines and grasses neatening her grave. Marking her plot with stones and rocks, I placed a large footrest at her feet, and straightened her cross. Each day I returned to dig with a kitchen knife, a spoon a fork. "Don't worry, I'll soon have you spruced up." I conmforted.

"Who was Emmy?" I asked our landlady and everyone I met.

"Oh some woman artist who lived down in the village years ago."

"An American tourist," nodded the owner of the village store.

"A poet," avowed another. Waiters, café and restaurant proprietors—not one of their answers sat easy. I became obsessed. Emmy. I tried imagining her tragedy, her death.

On my last week visiting the hacienda of a longtime Yelapa resident. I asked, "Do you know who Emmy was?"

"Emmy? Yes. He was Ralph Waldo Emerson's grandson. A great artist and poet. Gay. Too much prejudice in the States back then. Here he lived openly with his lover for over fifteen years. He was quite a celebrity. Shame. He got sick, wasted away and eventually died. He's buried in an old graveyard on the hill."

I hurried through the jungle. So that was it. Emmy wanted people to know Emmy was a he, that Emmy was no girl. Emmy was a man.

I searched for and found a wind-bleached plank of wood beside the fence. Lightly penciling lines, and pressing the stain from my marker pen, copied a quote of his from the New Yorker article I'd carried on the plane.

NATURE
ALWAYS
WEARS
THE
COLOR
OF
THE
SPIRIT

Ralph Waldo Emerson. Grandfather to his beloved grandson Emmy.

I felt him leave. Emmy didn't call again. At peace, his spirit left the desolation of the graveyard and vanished to wherever spirits go.

***D**avid's medical practice closed. I gave up sculpture. No past, no future, only the present existed. His caregiver, I gave up my life for his.*

Rather than us travel, for a change David and I decided it was time for my family to visit us in New Mexico so they and David could get to know one another a little more.

IT'S HOT ENOUGH

"Hey David," you ran to the living room from your office. "We'd better get planning. Miles and Kate are coming to visit us in September with the grandkids. They've accumulated enough air miles from his paper-recycling job to pay for the round trip. All four of tickets." Your words tumbled you were so excited. That's when the brainwave struck you.

"Instead of flying into Albuquerque, why not fly into Phoenix and make the journey here a one-way trip? The Painted Desert, fossilized Dinosaur footprints, Hot springs, Navajo ruins… maybe a roadrunner crossing the road. There's so much to see."

You recalled your own first impressions of the Southwest, the freedom of driving unbroken waves of rolling highway, as one-hundred and fifty-mile views stretched before you uncluttered by a single house or tree. Passing Saguaro cactus posed arms raised, instinctively you'd waved. Pulling off the road to stare in wonder at the lone, ship-like rocks jutting from the red sand you'd only seen in cowboy movies, a come-to-life cartoon Roadrunner, neck stretched, scuttled to escape my wheels. And then, there'd been the beckoning oases of shimmering water and palm trees, the first mirages you'd ever seen. Oh yes, they must see it all.

As you re-read the email message aloud, you could already feel your arms around them and smell the fresh greenness of them as you kissed their velvet-skinned English apple cheeks.

Catching a glimpse of your own wrinkled sun-aged arms, you shivered. Made a face. The twenty years since you had flown across the pond and immigrated to the Land of the Free, the dry New Mexican high desert had robbed every vestige of the rose complexion you'd arrived with.

"Wonderful news," David hugged me. "With the Highlander's two extra pop-up seats behind the back row, we can all squeeze in. Let's plan one trip at least. Hasn't it been nearly four years since they were here with us in Galisteo?"

You smiled. Your American husband loved both your sons, Anthony in England and in France, Miles, loved Kate your best daughter-in-law-in-all-the-world, as his own children. Grown up in single parent homes, David was both the beloved father to Miles and Kate, and adored Grandpa to their children. You watched the slight tremble of his hands, the pleasure spreading across your David's face.

"Are you poorly?" Five-year-old, Alfie, had queried staring up, his tiny hands resting on his Grandpa's knees.

"Grandpa has Parkinson's," I explained when my grandson shook imitating his involuntary movements soon after David had been diagnosed.

"These are the golden years," you'd comforted your David when could no longer practice medicine. "We can still live life to the full."

And carrying the Parkinson's thief on their backs, so far you and David had done just that. You'd walked hand-in-hand on the golden Malabar sands of the Indian ocean; suffered oil baths and enemas in an Ayurvedic clinic, Kerala; worshiped at the feet of a fifty-foot granite Buddhas reposed in each of the seven-tiered caves carved from the hillside, Sri Lanka; gawped at the leaning Tower of Pisa, explored the Haute Savoir in the French Alps, and sampled tapas in Northern Spain. Yes, the two of you had crammed in as many experiences as you could both digest.

"While we can," you'd both agreed. He'd hugged you, kissed

away the tear trickling from your eye.

Your head began to buzz with plans. Entertaining a six, and eight-year-old would be a challenge.

E-mails, phone calls, two months flew.

You packed. David snagged a roof-rack from E-bay for the extra luggage. I counted pills. Carbo-leva dopa, pills for Dyskinesia, pink and yellow ones, enough, and a few extra, for the week you'd be away. Cold box, ice packs, bottled water, potato chips, apples, a packet of trail mix. And this… Slipping in a small box of a secret something wrapped in wads of kitchen paper you closed the lid.

"Got everything?" and sliding into the driver's seat, you automatically leaned over and clicked your husband's seatbelt into place. Too difficult for him, you had taken over many simple tasks requiring fine-skill co-ordination.

One way to learn patience you muttered when you first realized how much the disease had slowed him down.

"Why don't you take over from me once we're on the open road?" I suggested not wanting to dent his eroding confidence.

On high alert, eyes semi-closed you pretended to rest for the hour he took over the wheel. It was all you could do not to grab the steering wheel and scream stop, stop.

After a night at the motel recovering from the drive, and way too early, you'd sped to the Skyport, and scanned each LANDED announcement for their flight.

"Hello my Darlings. At last, you're here. Welcome. Welcome," How you shrieked hugging and smothering your bedraggled family with kisses, when you spied them grouped around the baggage carousel in 'Arrivals.'

Heat and distance are what we English long for, sun hot enough to fry an egg, and empty roads disappearing to vanishing point. Ecstatic, for two full days your son Miles, his lovely Kate, and young grandchildren swam aquatic dolphin feats, hiked the cooler morning desert among the Arizonan cactus until their fair skin roasted-red. And when evening came, sipped salt-rimmed margaritas and American root beer in air-conditioned sunsets, double-dipping unfamiliar Nacho chips in salsa and guacamole.

The car ready loaded, Miles in the driver's seat, our trip home was about to begin. You studied their five faces. If you had to choose just one word to describe your smiling family, yes, happy would be the word. Suddenly sad, but for how much longer, I wondered.

"Granny has a surprise," you announced gaily. "Before we head for home and leave the desert, who'd like to fry an egg on a rock? OK then, let's do it."

"Voilà." You crowed producing the egg from the cold-box, the raw egg you nursed five days and carried from New Mexico for exactly this.

"And here to fry it…" you added, "three butter-pats pocketed from our motel breakfast. All you need now is to find a flat-topped rock."

The sun in its zenith, the stark hills above Phoenix faded hazy in the heat. We chose a suitable rock and crowded round, cameras pointed ready. The butter sizzled.

"One! Two! Three! Now, Miles, now!" We chorused.

Cameras whirred. He tapped it open on a rock. The cracked egg slithered through the butter. It landed into the dirt un-fried.

Oh, how we laughed. So that's how you fry an egg is it? We teased and laughed five hundred miles home.

$\mathcal{G}$oddammit, now I can't even chew my food," he cursed. "Another symptom of Parkinson's disease, I need to find an orthodontist."

When David smiled, instead of pearly whites, he revealed a scattering of brown points.

NO LAUGHING MATTER

Dentists are no laughing matter …. until they present you with their bill, that is. Do they see gold bars inside a mouth? A Picasso canvas doesn't fetch as much per inch as teeth framed alluringly in gums. With just twelve stubs remaining, Richard's situation was dire. Something needed doing if he wasn't to waste away, forever limited to a liquid diet.

Returning from consultations with several recommended dental experts in his state, he reported,

"$50,000 for the implants…. um….," He hesitated seeing his wife's jaw slacken, her eyes jam wide, "….without the crowns or X-rays, and then I'll need…."

She didn't let him finish. Lydia leaped to her feet. "Are they 'barking'? Pull out the lot … wear a plate…fit wooden teeth like George Washington." Sparks scorched the estimate in her husband's hand. "For that price, we could buy a B.M.W. or cruise the world!" Lydia's face reddened. "Do the bastards expect us to take out a second mortgage?! The world's gone mad!"

Lydia pictured Eduardo, the hard-working day laborer she'd hired the previous week, grateful for every dollar bill he earned from hacking through the frozen earth in search of a buried pipe, then his delighted surprise for the gas money she'd added to his hourly rate. She saw their elderly neighbor's tireless caregiver, exhausted and unpaid. Heard the teachers' battling cries as they fed overflowing classrooms of hungry minds. She bled for every honest worker indentured to a wage.

"It's a puzzle. What to do?" Defeated, Richard shook his head.

"Dental Tourism! That's the answer! I've read about it somewhere."

Google research revealed a host of choices, Thailand, Bulgaria, Costa Rica, India and Mexico, among many others. 'Nearest is best,' they both agreed. 'Mexico will suit.' Pouring over websites Richard and Lydia judged clinics by their advertised specialties, and their command of English. E-mails hummed in cyberspace.

"Puerto Vallarta. A long established American and Canadian wintering-hole for Snowbirds and retirees owning second homes. An ocean resort on the 'holiday package' route, perfect! No way those people would put up with shoddy work. They'd demand standards comparable to ours," they argued. Rightly so, they discovered.

Richard and Lydia burrowed in the storage boxes of their shed, packed their bags; light summer clothes, swimming togs, sunscreen, and boogie board. They waved the snow-threatening sky goodbye and headed for the sun and salty sea. Moisture. Warmth. The very thought of those two words had their desiccated skin hydrating. Living in the high, mountain desert of New Mexico, they dreamed humidity.

The hotel hugged the beach. Their room opened onto a bougainvillea-edged balcony overlooking a bay from where they watched a school of dolphins leap towards the setting sun. They walked the sand at dawn. Breakfasted on ripe papaya. Dipping 'totopos' chips in spicy guacamole, a salt-rimmed glass of margarita in their hands, Happy Hour was 'Happy Hour' every hour, everyday.

A Canadian in the dentist's waiting room started chatting. Lydia and Richard's guarded expressions advertised newcomer's fears. "You've come to the best dentist in all of Mexico." His smile flashed a reassuring set of pearly whites. "My wife and I come every winter."

The sunlit room gleamed, polished. The toilet flushed. A sculptured basin in the restroom ran hot and cold. Dental assistants' matching uniforms rustled, comfortingly crisp. Digital computer screens stood by every chair. Lydia counted; one dentist for root canals, one for extractions and a third for gum surgery.

"At your age and with your health issues," they advised Richard, "We suggest the less invasive, less expensive treatment of posts and crowns."

Spread over the following three weeks, Richard endured eight appointments grunting, "Ah! Ha! Ah! Ha!" in response to the dentist's "You doing OK? Like a five-minute break?"

"You need a bone graft back there," Dr Mauricio tapped the spot. "... to save that molar."

"No way! Pull the thing out." Lydia sat up, ripped off her bib and fled the dental chair.

An appointment later, it was the extraction specialist's turn. "I'm not pulling out a good tooth," he said. "What you need is a bone graft."

"But ... the bone... where does come from?" Lydia flustered without giving him time to answer. "... a chicken leg? ... my thigh?" Once his laughter subsided, "Its synthetic. Comes from Geneva in a little vial. Implanted, bone grows into it compensating for the loss. I'm told my hands are the gentlest in Mexico. Don't worry. I'll make sure you'll feel no pain."

At least thinking that was what he said, Lydia agreed. He was right, there was no pain. She asked for the shorter lasting anesthetic so she could sip a banana smoothie all the sooner without drooling. A pillow beneath her head, supine in the dental chair, Vaseline on her lips, but for the brief sting as of a bee, Lydia floated painless from beneath eye shades, while soft hands probed, drilled and did what dentists do. The stitches came out in a week. The bone graft 'took' holding the molar firm.

Those visits were the down side of their holiday, those, and days consuming dreary bowls of soup while gums healed.

The final visit arrived, squeezed into their last day. Richard smiled a Hollywood smile sporting nineteen 'gnashers.' Mis-planning, they'd not allowed enough time to complete the work. "It takes a month for the gums to shrink to size. You'll need to return," Dr. Mauricio insisted.

'Two more 'hard' weeks in the sun. Poor things! Such hardship!' Friend's eyes narrow, green. "We're Mexico bound again. Found a great off-season package deal."

Back in the U.S., Richard's temporary crowns came unglued due to excessive flossing. Cost for a ten-minute visit; the equivalent of half a porcelain crown, or eight panoramic X-rays, or five dental cleanings, (dentist's inspection included) in Puerta Vallarta.

Laugh! Oh how Richard and Lydia laughed before they cried. Rolling his eyes, Richard nibbled rabbit teeth at Lydia while signing his credit card. They began giggling.

"Dental tourism works for us," they tell friends. "No question."

*D*avid stared at himself in the bathroom mirror. Flashed a toothy smile.

"Something's different. You're looking great," friends now greeted.

"Yes, doesn't he look good? I chime in giving David a look, not explaining his nineteen posts and crowns. Grace a our dentist in Puerta Vallarta.

One thousand greenbacks down, titanium partials filled in the few remaining gaps. Snap, snap, he practiced before making light work of his New York steak as if it were soft cheese.

I never did like the things, though. Something about the way the teeth stared back grinning from a tooth-mug made me flinch each time.

GRANDPA'S TEETH

"I need a box for my teeth," Grandpa announced forcibly from the family car's front seat pulling out his "partials."

The family exiting the car froze in mid-gather—bathing towels, bucket and spade, two sets of flippers, snorkels, rolled up beach umbrella, fishing rod, suntan cream, hats and...

"I don't want them to come loose in the sea." Grandpa sat firm, the car door open.

"My sunglasses case might work." Daughter-in-law plumped down the cooler offering the transparent case.

Grandpa looked doubtful and opened his mouth to protest, but kept silence on catching Grandma's glare.

Snatching both upper and lower sets she tucked one either side of the nose divider inside the spectacle case. Thirteen teeth, pink plastic gums, a titanium brace glinted through its plexi.

"Perfect," Grandma nodded dropping them into her bag. "Safe as houses."

And so followed a happy day at the French Mediterranean seaside.

A replica of Neptune and his trident, Grandpa perched himself on a rock and gazed out to sea, immobile, clutching the umbrella pole, a spread towel across his knees chasing shade.

"But its warm once you're in," Grandma and Daughter-in-law cajoled waist deep in the water splashing enticingly.

Grandpa pursed his lips, dug his toes deep into the sand and shook his head. Just then a gust of wind flipped the umbrella into the air twisting its ribs inside out. Grandpa making a grab for it toppled sideways and fell grazing his leg. Scrambling to his aid the family propped him back, weighted the umbrella with stones, and calmed him with a coke from the cooler. Five times the red, white and blue thing took flight forcing them to abandon the beach. Packed, they struggled back up the cliff path to the car.

Grandma burrowed in her bag.

"Here." She said from the back seat passing Grandpa's teeth to him over his left shoulder.

Everybody recalled that last sighting in the car's grocery store parking lot before driving the two-miles to Leucate's cliff-top lighthouse for an evening stroll.

"Oh look. Bottoms," giggled 14 year-old Granddaughter, ogling a shoal of male nudists bobbing in the sea four hundred feet below the rim's overlook Grandma adjusted her specs for a better view.

The sun lowered, raked Anjou-rose-wine furrows across the sky calling them to head for home.

Seated round the patio table back at their rented house, while the children cavorted in the swimming pool, the four adults sipped Muscat followed by Fitou from a local vineyard, enhanced the wines' bouquet by snacking olives, squares of goat Tomme, and marinated anchovies while the barbecue grill came to heat.

"Supper," Son called spearing a lamb chop.

"Forgot my teeth." Grandpa disappeared into his room, returned harried.

Problem. Gawn. Vanished.

A grand hunt ensued. Poking, peering, lifting, tipping, emptying, shaking—car seats, beach bags, towels, pockets—nothing was left undisturbed. Not on the driveway, in the house or car, they were nowhere to be found. Dusk prevented further search, though Grandma and Daughter-in-law continued pulling open every drawer in their minds.

Sleep came fitfully. $1,000 dollar bills tossed and surged loss and replacement. With the dawn a plan emerged: retrace and search every stopping place since Grandpa's teeth were last seen.

Nine o'clock next morning, the Grocery store car lot shone mirror smooth—empty.

Making out a report, the Policewoman at the Station tittering behind her hand to cover her smile so infuriated Grandma she snapped her seat belt undone and made to jump out of the car and slog her one, growling,

browlin in English, "It's not funny, bitch," which the female Gendarme happily didn't catch.

"Please, please, Grandma, just forget it." Granddaughter pleaded placing a restraining hand on Grandma's arm. "Please don't cause any trouble."

"Lighthouse. One last place." Daughter-in-law asserted. "We'll look there."

At the cliff-top, the family fanned out across the stony terrain in the approximate vicinity where they'd parked the previous evening. In less than a minute, Son brandished aloft the crushed remnants of the spectacle case.

Run-over, squelched flat, two sets of teeth gleamed visible coated in grime. Was it possible they'd survived? Granddaughter emptied a bottle of drinking water and wiped them clean. Crowding round, six pairs of eyes watched riveted. Between thumb and forefinger, taking each in turn, Grandpa slipped them over his gums snapping them in place. He gnashed his teeth and grinned. But for one small tweak of one strand of wire, a perfect fit.

Moral: travel with your snappers in a box.

*B*ehavioral and physical changes like his inde-cipherable writing, evermore frequent stumbles, fading memory, curving posture, loomed, threat-ening, from the future. Already I feeling the Parkinsonian sea rippling into our lives, I shiver. Wish we were young again holding hands stroll-ing the Malabar coast and riding waves twenty feet high in the Indian Ocean, and dream of for the ever and ever that can never be.

One day our village mailman delivered a let-ter, no return address, no signature. It's writing obviously disguised. DOCTOR DAVID, the enve-lope read. The message inside so shocking, I hid it from David. I burned it before he could see it.

If Parkinson's doesn't kill you, I will.

How dare you interfere in our marriage, I screamed at the sender banging open his front door, for I knew very well who'd scribed such venom.

WATER'S EDGE

"Café Circus," Ellen paused at the water's edge. A circular building stood marooned across a mudslide. She was to meet Phil for coffee there at nine. Early, her watch read ten to. A surging spate now raged where black tarmac should have been.

Out of the dim past, Phil, an old and long discarded friend, had called her up two days before. They hadn't spoken in …was it eight…eleven years?

"It's urgent," he whispered down the phone. "I have something to return to you that was never mine. Something I took… err..um stole from your husband Jeff, and must return," is all he muttered.

"Café Circus? Tuesday at 9am, then," reluctant Ellen agreed.

"Meeting a friend for coffee," she called to her husband, Jeff and banged the door headed for the rendezvous.

She'd listened to the night's rainstorm's pounding the leaves outside her bedroom, then soften to a pattering drizzle with the morning light.

Grey-black clouds hugged the mountain-top. The night's torrential rain had forced debris through the arroyo beds so fast, the parched earth within them churned to mud. She hesitated. Should she take a step, wade out to where the footing lay unseen? And as she paused, the tip of Circus Café's tent-like tin roof tipped launching the entire building downstream point first. Rearing up from the water's surface, then settling down as the building bobbed passed her like a toy boat. Ellen froze

"Step back." A megaphone blared making her along with the

gaping crowd, leap back.

"No. My-god, and ahhs," reverberated through the watching crowd and held her as turning she watched a human chain of emergency workers pull bodies from the water and load black plastic body-bag after body-bag to the waiting ambulances.

"Fatalities all from Café Circus. None were saved." Ellen nodded, acknowledging the whispers of the crowd.

Did one of those fatalities include Phil, the old friend she had arranged to meet? The man she had sworn to never speak or see ever again. Why ever hadf she agreed to meet him and break her vow? She asked herself bitterly.

Ellen remembered back. Mean memories rattled, scrabbled at her brain as the past surfaced. Brutal. The anonymous poison Phil penned in a letter to her Parkinson's suffering husband, Jeff. The alarm, hearing from a trusted girlfriend, his hate-letter was on its way.

"...although I promised never to tell, I just have to warn you. Phil has written Jeff an anonymous letter. It's pretty nasty." Her friend warned.

Ice-shards splintered. Newly diagnosed and already fragile, she feared her beloved Jeff would snap.

Ellen remembered her desperate daily runs to intercept the mail before... she shuddered, reliving the what-if of his reading it. Jeff, her husband. Three days she waited.

Going for the mail, she waved cheerily. For three days she sped the 1,000 feet of drive to their roadside mailbox, snatched the contents, shuffled through the day's delivery.

If she didn't intercept it first, its verbal poison could push him over reason's edge—his hope for life dashed. Back then Jeff still floundered, adjusting to his disease. The decline ahead. The steady loss of body and intellectual control. Phil's vitriol was sure to have found its mark.

Ellen's forehead wrinkled. Her lips thinned, compressed.

Relief. Dread. The third afternoon it was there, the letter. Its scrawled red ink across the envelope addressed "King Tut" alerted. Her hand shook as she stuffed it over her heart into the lace cup of her bra.

For a day she deliberated. Burn it sight unseen. It's foul words un-spilled. Open it? Don't? To read or not to read? Tell him? Not tell? Questions swilled unanswered.

Ellen sat crossed-legged before a low table in the quietness of her bedroom. Lit the candle. Three times tapped the singing bowl, waved an incense stick releasing Champa and the bowl's song to the unseen, she offered up the envelope.

"…glad you're sick…if your disease wasn't going to kill you, I would come out with a knife and kill you myself…hope you suffer…"

The inked words smudged.

"How dare you strike when a man is down…what could you have been thinking to have done such a wicked thing." Ellen's anger battered, bursting into Phil's house the next day.

Ellen remembered screaming, slamming his door never to see or hear from the man again. And hadn't. Yet.

What had barbed Phil's mind? Twisted it against her gentle husband, Jeff. She never did discover.

Ellen mulled over past interactions between the two. Phil and Jeff. When she married Jeff, had he felt supplanted? Feared their marriage would rob him of his and Ellen's closeness? She knew Phil once tried to wheedle her MD husband into prescribing him painkillers for recreational use. Was Jeff's sharp refusal the big offence that speared their bond, turned him from friend to a foe?

She had no answer.

Eight years of mutual silence had passed. Though they inhabited the same small town, there had been not one sighting. Then the phone call…. Café Circus? Nine am? And so it was arranged.

Ellen brought her attention to the flood. It's rising waters swept past wetting her toes. She looked at her watch. Still no Phil. She turned and walked for home.

A week later, Fed-ex delivered a brown envelope stamped with a Government seal addressed to her husband Jeff.

"This package was recovered from the pocket of one deceased, Phil D. Please sign acknowledging receipt and return in the enclosed," the official note read.

Inside the small package, a crumpled sheet of words all but washed away inside a plastic sandwich baggie. Holding the note to the light, Ellen deciphered just one phrase from its scrawl.

"…stealing from you what you planned on giving Ellen, I hoped to keep her for myself…regret…Phil."

A sparkling diamond ring fell onto the tablecloth. Jeff's and Ellen's jaws dropped. Their eyes opened wide.

"What the devil…? Jeff exclaimed. "That's Mother's diamond engagement ring. The ring I planned to give you the day we married, the one I could never find. How the dickens…?"

David's Parkinson's disease weighed heavy. Too heavy now for David to ever be left on his own. Too heavy to eat in public...drive a car...press his finger to the TV control button...dial the phone... turn the pages of a book.

We gave away his Kindle to a friend. Burrowing into the past we recalled our do-you-remember-when... stories.

I kept a bright face of course, didn't voice my dread. But come night, terrors filled my dreams. Jumbled, tortuous, uncontrolled, elusive, sometimes me, sometimes a boy child, running, running, chasing, never capturing time.

TIME

I have Grandpa to thank for my lifelong obsession with watches. Inevitable, like the passing of the present to the past, I became a clock man when I grew up.

"A memento. Keep this and yourself wound and ticking, dear little fellow. There's no hurry. I'll be here waiting when it is your time."

Mother handed me a small cardboard box. Inside, a note—spidery letters penned in pale blue ink, a green baize bag holding his pocket watch and chain, Grandpa's Elgin wristwatch, and the porcelain miniature of my Granma, Rosalind. Pointing to tiny, italic phosphorescent numbers on the watch dial, not understanding then the workers who hand-painted them so dainty, so perfect, died of throat and lip cancer from sucking the coated squirrel-hair brushes to the finest point, Mother said I couldn't wear the watch until I learned what time its two hands told.

I was seven when Grandpa died. Called to his heavenly abode, Mother said.

Seeing Grandpa's grave buried beneath a mound of sweet flowers, convinced me he was om his second honeymoon in the Himalayan Valley of the Flowers with his Rosalind—the valley he'd often told me of where, so overcome by its beauty and heady perfumed flowers, Rosalind, had swooned. But I was a little cross, and cried and cried. He'd left me behind and hadn't taken me with him.

"Grandpa, do you have a watch inside you? *Dumbv-dumbv-dumbv.* I can hear ticking."

Snuggled on Grandpa's lap, I leaned back, my ear pressing against the softness of his velvet waistcoat. "Tick. Tick. Tick…."

"It's self-winding." He ruffled my hair and laughed. "You, Mummy, everyone, animals too, all have their own ticker. One that keeps on going until it's time for it to stop."

Grandpa fumbled in one of the two small pockets in his yellow waistcoat then made a play of reeling in the chain draped across his belly-bulge.

"Hey presto. Look I've hooked." He cried, and fishing out his gold timepiece, dangled his catch before me like a trout.

"Go on little fellow. Follow the moving hand with your eyes and count. Tick. Tock…."

"….ninety-nine, one hundred." We exploded together triumphant as if we'd summited the highest mountain peak.

"Now, shut your eyes. Count using only your ears." The watch pressed to my ear—the faintest tick tickled.

After our counting game, Grandpa slid the watch-end of the chain back out of sight into the left pocket with his right hand.

Grandpa and I were best friends. Me, five, and he eighty plus years.

We often sat together. Grandpa in his smoking chair. Me comfy on his knee, my head against his chest. His habit was to encourage me to finger-walk my way along the watch chain's watch to its end, then gently probe for the hidden treasure inside the other pocket. Smaller, lighter in weight, engraved with leaves and blossoms intertwined, the gold oval disc no bigger than a flattened pigeon's egg, I handed back to him.

"Let's say hello to Grandma." Grandpa flipped the lid. "Hello, my dear," he whispered to the young women painted there inside the frame. Her cheeks blushed pink, a half-smile playing on her lips she looked as if she had just woken from her beauty sleep.

Grandpa said I had her eyes. "Very rare." He said, "Blue as

the Himalayan poppies." Grandpa told me he and Grandma and had discovered high in the mountains while hiking in the Valley of the Flowers.

"Ahh. The most beautiful place in all the world…" Grandpa paused, his eyes misty. "Your Grandpa and Grandma," he murmured, "lay down right there to rest beneath the sky surrounded by snow crusted mountains with wildflowers for our bed, so scented four hours passed as two."

"Go on Grandpa, tell me more, the bit about the tigers."

They were on their honeymoon round the world, I knew that. They'd sailed from England's docklands following the sun— Italy, Madeira, then around the horn of Africa to a French spice island called Reunion. From there they crossed the Indian Ocean to wander in the bamboo forest of Lord Mountbatten's botanical gardens of Ceylon before they set ever foot on India's Malabar Coast at the ancient port of Cochin. Grandpa's stories filled me with longing to see for myself tigers, elephants, peacocks and waterfalls ten stories high and drink milk that came from coconuts not cows. And most of all I wanted to see a Pipol tree. People? I wanted to see a People tree.

Through his eyes I dined on quail stuffed with tamarind served on silver platters placed before me by men in scarlet, liveried uniforms. I lounged on silk cushions beside a be-jeweled Maharaja and Maharani dripping ruby, sapphire and emerald gems, and pearls the size of kumquats, hypnotized by green and scarlet faces of Katak dancers.

"I'll let you go now my darling. Farewell Rosalind, until it is my time to join you in your heavenly abode." Grandpa's voice wavered. His whiskers trembled.

Grandpa said my time was a long, long way off, when I asked if I could go to see her too.

For a few years following Grandpa's departure for his second honeymoon in a place Mummy always called a heavenly abode, I jumped whenever I heard her call, "Time. It's time to…"

But the call was always only for my evening bath, for meals, for bed, and to stop my noisy playing.

With more important things to do than mourn, my memory of Grandpa receded. Sometimes after I fell asleep, I saw him sitting on a dream earth mound amongst the flowers reaching his open hands to receive me tousling my hair. Then he'd tap his wrist in reminder of the hour and mime shooing me away back home on earth. Pointing his index finger back behind me he'd shake his head. "No, dear boy not your time, not yet."

You know you'll have to put him in a home one day, don't you? His sister's harsh statement gripped my heart. No way. Never. Never would I ever, ever allow that, to be David's fate I screamed, having seen my gentle Stepmother wither away in what I call an end-of-life facility.

LIFE SENTENCE

dread pass through massive gates grip the steering wheel park enter reception

the inner door is locked

visiting? *Susan*

time? *10.15 am*

sign-in *Liz* scrawl my name

ring the bell wait

you are to be taken from here to a secure place to serve out your term

your sentence life without parole

pardon for which the woman pleaded refused

four years passed

hers confined mine spanned continents a new marriage candle-lit dinners

a smattering of Japanese learned from Duolingo on my cell phone

bolts being drawn keys turned crash me to the present

yes? a face queries

I'm here to see Susan, I say.

find her eyes closed nestled with a clutch of other white-haired inmates waiting for the one-eyed ogre blaring from the wall to cease its relentless barrage

to keep your skin youthful...wrinkle free

a lip-sticked blonde plugs beauty tips unaware on whose ears her garbage falls

five faces gaze tentative plead

me have you come to visit me wordless for a second twenty
eyes sparkle

is it me is it me is it me will I be it the chosen one?

pale cheeks firm with hopeful smiles sag as I pass

it's you I stop

Susan lifts her head

scrape lift clunk scrape-clunk rubber tips green linoleum her
walker inches headed for her room one young one old slowly we
walk

she gives a mighty hawk splat a glob hits green

Susan you can't do that I reprove aghast

shhh she whispers don't tell

her eyes light up glint she smiles

settles on embroidered scarlet poppies cushioning her chair

I'm 99 you know coy Susan lies adds two years

briefly her head sinks uncurls from her baby-blue blouse like
a snail from her shell

how lovely to see you darling where is it you live now? her face brightens

mother daughter we hold hands squeeze petal so soft rub
rough bark

deep pools we swim

I can't believe it you're really here her eyes hold mine

questions answers repeat words circle fresh as if spoken for
the first time

unfolding her life from within two sheets of paper written
years before I read to her

her own story the story she wants read at her funeral

Susan Sclater born 1914 in The Close... torpedoed I never
knew my Admiral father...became a Red Cross nurse... ban-
daged wounded troops...Algeria...no map...ordered to drive a
ten-ton lorry to Anzio...my friend Joyce... so cold, we needed
woolen skirts.

really? I did all those things?
you remember Wuzzer my terrier don't you Liz? memories wander
it was before my time I say
five six seven times and yet again I read aloud
hungry Susan drinks in every word till finally she's sated
Susan never looked up when I kissed her goodbye and left her
room weeping
in the corridor outside her door a woman clutches at my sleeve
help I need help perhaps you can tell me
I should be home what am I doing I here

I am not his mother. Don't want to be. Never have been. Nor for that matter his sister. Standing behind him, I slide my arms under his. Encircle him. He turns to hug remembering belly touching belly. I nibble the underside of his neck. He blows a raspberry between my breasts.

In sickness and in health, we laugh suddenly in love again. I'm sorry I yelled, my darling. I just can't function on three hours sleep.

Is there no relief, no end to our suffering? How much longer can we both go on?

I began a blog. A blog for Caregiver's in support of their suffering, for I'd found nothing to support the hell I was going through. For eighteen months, every week, I spilled my woes for all to see.

A logical step, already written, my blog became book.

THE PERFECT SERVANT...
NOPE

blog post January 21, 2017

THE BLUE HOLE... 90 MILES AHEAD

Driving home from a blogging class in Albuquerque one day last fall I passed a billboard on Route 66.

"LESS THAN TWO HOURS TO YOUR JOURNEY'S END. THE BLUE HOLE—90 MILES AHEAD," proclaimed the advertisement of the local tourist attraction where without success scuba divers have sought its source.

The image of swimming through the Blue Hole's watery lens to infinity put me in mind of death.

Can you imagine, Caregivers, knowing your journey's end? Would knowing be a death sentence or relief? I imagined life shrinking, crossing off each day until none remained but one final sunset before embarking on a final mystery journey.

Would we, should we, weep for another year of life gone by? 10–9–8—as we do when the New Year's ball begins its drop, then exchange kisses and rejoice...

HAPPY NEW YEAR. HAPPY NEW LIFE.

I imagine the agony of the terminally ill sentenced to a certain number of days of life, a prisoner counting hours one by one to—barbaric murder to my mind–execution.

I can't decide if knowing would collapse the two of us crazy with grief, or cinch us more tightly to each other. I can't decide if I would cram our last days doing all the things we'd wished to do but have never done.

My wish: hold hands with David watching dawn streak crimson-gold over the Taj Mahal.

David's: France beside me on a pew bathed together in the rainbow-colored light of La Rochelle's stained glass windows.

Maybe we'd give away everything we owned. Maybe stay right here in the house we built and love?

To know or not to know your journey's end date? That is the question. Love to hear what you think caregivers. If it's a dilemma you grapple with. Coping with "End of life planning?"

Loss came the answer. Devastating sense of loss. Weird after all my moaning how exhausting I found caregiving.

The phone rang yesterday. "This is George, your best friend."

I knew no George and was about to punch disconnect when he added, "Your husband stopped by at my stand at the Albuquerque Parkinson's Conference last week requesting information on pre-paid cremation."

So many stalls, so many leaflets touting different information, the day's talks pushing alternative therapies of all the must dos we could-should be doing, the conference left me depressed if I am honest.

It wasn't the sight of so many gimped up people and their captive gaolers that punctured my spirit, no—it was the word hope.

"Never give up hope." The keynote speaker dunked the word HOPE to the audience. Dunked a new word for me, I pitched it to a corner of my mind.

The key-note speaker, star basketball athlete Brian Grant, introduced a video of him dunking ball after ball. Six foot nine, Rasta hair, a startlingly beautiful face, and perfectly proportioned body, he held the mike.

A flash of light caught my eye. The shifting sparkle of the

diamonds framing his wristwatch jiggled, thrown by his tremor. A vice-grip of realization cramped my insides.

"This gorgeous chunk of humanity suffers from PD" I whispered to David. "So young." Was it all the more cruel because he was in his thirties, I questioned.

Early onset PD, Brian informed us. I can play before a stadium of tens of thousands no problem, but you lot, an audience of fellow sufferers and caregivers has me shaking like a leaf." He paused laughing and plunged his tremoring hand deep into his pocket, hoping against hope to hide it.

"Never give up hope." I never thought I'd climb a mountain, he looked directly at us. I and five other PD sufferers, he used the acronym for Parkinson's, conquered Mount St Helens last summer. Hell of a struggle but we all made it to the summit.

His saying don't give up is when I realized hope is exactly what I had surrendered. No cure, the caterpillar-like disease relentlessly biting chunks from David's and my lives. That was a day I was stuck. Depressed. Convinced we'd never to morph to butterflies.

"You never asked for this, caregivers," the speaker continued.

Turning to us, the audience, he asked, "Any caregivers out there? Put your hands up. Thank you," he said. "Thank you," he repeated adding you never asked for Parkinson's to be in your life, but everyone of you is suffering from Parkinson's too. "You were never asked to give up your lives to caregiving, but you did. Thank you, I thank every one of you."

It was then I started to cry. David apart, it was the first time I felt truly acknowledged, the first time anyone directly beamed deep gratitude from their heart.

Wearing hope's face mask when my insides are dust is hard. Hope is my only staff. Hope is what buoys me afloat. If hope slips away, what then…

... those days I find him slumped hollow-eyed a sand-dried carcass like the Red-tailed Hawk remains we came upon together walking barefoot in White Sands National Monument... those days like today when he sits slumped at breakfast one cheek hard pressed to the table, left arm hanging from the chair, fingers reaching the floor—beneath his cheek, a flattened muffin...

... those days I sink into the fathomless waters of the Blue Hole, wonder how long can I cope with him at home, those days I cry, "Help me make it through today."

"You realize he'll have to go into a home one day."

She, of all people, his sister, a geriatric nurse—is she nuts? Could a tortoise gouged from his shell keep living? Could David? Only if and when, like the poor buggers incapacitated, too aged, too financially strapped with no-one, then I suppose, social services would insist he be taken into care. Bodily bundle him away.

But today David is ON enough to insist, "I'm begging you to see to it, Liz. Don't let them invade my right to stay home with you."

"You realize he'll have to go into a home, one day." His sister and her nurse-friend reiterated.

"He can just as well be a vegetable here in his own chair, if that's what he becomes." I countered frostily. "Paying for home care costs the same as a facility. I'll never let him die alone in some awful institution. NEVER."

Affirmed in love, occasionally repented in exhaustion, those days a scream rips, "I can't go on. I can't." I do and can of course. The same way I dragged from bed fevered and weak to tend my children many years ago.

"Better to die than come to that—go into a home." My husband had sworn. "I'll do away with myself."

A doctor—he surely squirreled a stash of knockout pills in a place only he knew. Don't tell. Don't ask. I never have.

I didn't sleep well that night for a nightmare of my David crumpled lopsided in a cage. Me passing spiked carrots and bananas to him through the bars. Me dragged away in handcuffs charged with murder. Last sight of him, an abandoned family pet in the pound, the pleading in his eyes.

I woke with the image nailed to my visual cortex.

"I love you so much," Planting kisses on his head while handing him a breakfast cereal bowl, I guide a spoon into his fumbling fingers, my face averted.

Are you plagued by nightmares, caregivers? It's hard remembering they are not real. It's hard keeping strong.

"Don't crumble," I tell myself. "We have lots of normal moments to remember."

Like the many times David eats a meal without me having to spoon-feed him. Like the evenings spent quietly together in the back yard drinking up the Indian Summer sun watching the peach tree shred her golden leaves. I fall for it, every time... we are a married couple again living with hope. Normal.

It's hard being a caregiver, isn't it? A grey-haired woman in the car park tossed, as guiding her husband's shuffle towards their car, he dragged on her hand. Wild wisps, lost hope escape the pins holding her hair. Wrinkles rut her cheeks. Her body hollow from giving calls for comfort. When next I saw her months had passed. She walked alone. The playful blouse she wore, flounced skirt, and lipstick pearling her lips proclaimed freedom reclaimed. Would that be me when…?

KAFKA'S GRUB

Well it happened. A full time Caregiver, worn down by stress and round-the-clock caring, I've turned into a Kafka grub and people treat me as such although I reassure them, I am the same person who I was last month when they saw me as a humanoid with two eyes that fully opened and smooth furrowed skin covering my face. I fell you see. Smack-flat on my face trying to help David into the car.

I've always prided myself on my English complexion, my cheeks soft, moisturized by England's endless rain, that was until I glimpsed a monster grub illuminated by the bright light cast by six 'stage' bulbs aligned above my bathroom looking glass. I had no need to ask the mirror on the wall, as had the wicked witch in Snow White. I knew. I was not the fairest in the land.

Pomegranate red, the grub's crackled skin was peeling as mud lifts from a drought-stricken lake, its eyes glowing green pinpoints in the electric glare. I walked, talked and felt the same. Trouble was, people veered away slamming doors with expressions registering alarm as if whatever befell me might befall them too.

"He--ll---!" but they were already out of sight, gone, never to hear the 'o' which added to 'hell' becomes a friendly, 'He-llo!

I look in the mirror. Wild-haired, furrowed face, a crazed woman stares back. Me. Not crazed, I'm just a caregiver, I reassure.

Overnight we became personas non-fff-ing-grata, who nobody wanted to be around. Feared social pariahs to be avoided. And, if I'm honest, I wouldn't choose us either to take up space at a dinner table for six or eight—dead-weights with NEEDs who don't fan witty dinner conversation.

If friends do stop to say hello at a social gathering, How you doing? They ask moving along without waiting for your reply. Better make the rounds, they murmur making their escape.

BEE

It's been twenty years since the doctor in him died, since he discovered the Parkinson's thief shackled to his side, since he shut himself inside the hive at the end of his garden, and made it his home.

Sited on a rise among the purple flowering cholla, from the hive's opening he could see the sunrise spark Mount Baldy's snow peak fifty miles away, and watch the moon slide her light into the sky those nights he was wakeful.

Standing in the shaft of light he pruned his sprouting bee parts. He didn't have to beg his wife to join him, she just followed him inside and exchanged her dress for a fuzzy yellow pantsuit decorated with black stripes.

"For better or worse," she pronounced, "I'm here for you, my love."

She popped a glob of pollen under her tongue and puckered her lips.

Long abandoned by the previous occupants and with nobody to upbraid them, the couple let things slide. Beds stayed un-made, unwashed dishes piled precariously beside the sink, newspapers littered the floor and crammed the hollow spaces of the honeycomb. Of an evening, over a glass of dandelion or elderberry wine they laughed out loud pointing at the mess.

"Oh B-darling, (she called him by his new nickname) how even one year ago we'd have died of shame."

To make the point, she spat out a sunflower husk and shuffled it with her foot onto the pile collecting on the floor.

The first two years of retirement they were able to keep their secret hidden while they figured out how to adapt to their new bee way of living.

"We taking a long road trip," they lied to their friends.

The two of them mapped out a plan while their transformation took place—the time between human and bee when Dr. B's stomach-fur hadn't quite grown in, and wing buds still irritated Mrs. B's skin.

Though Dr. and Mrs. B pretended not to, their close friends noticed the new roundness of their bodies, glazed pupils, difficulty forming words, sudden reluctance to shake hands or exchange hugs, and noted the outright refusal to give out their new address. Whenever they did leave the house, they enveloped their fur, and extra budding legs and wings with padded jackets adding at least ten pounds to their appearance.

"My, don't we look plump," they had laughed poking a finger at the other's midriff.

It was one Saturday in January—the last time they ventured out socially.

"We won't take no for an answer. We insist you come," their good friends persuaded. "Rabbie Burns night. Someone is bringing his bagpipes."

Their hosts ignored their sloppy manners, Dr. B's tremoring, the spilled innards of the haggis and gravy from his fork, and the petit pois rolling across the table. As the flaming haggis was held aloft and piped in by a kilted piper and Dr. B raised his glass, his whiskey sloshed spattering the red and green tartan table cloth.

Staring at the stubble sprouted on the doctor's chin, their hostess marveled at how well they both looked, and the elegance of their matching black and lemon-yellow outfits.

"You look just like a pair of …." pushing away a strand of unwanted sentence her laugh smudged to a faint smile. The hostess ran her hand over her hair and fixed her eyes on a cobweb cornered by the ceiling.

Dr. B and Mrs. B caught one another' eyes. Though brief, the exchange told the other they could no longer risk exposure. Be seen in public.

The hum-mmm-ming surging from inside Dr. B became audible.

"Thank you. We need to be going." Too early and a little impolite to leave, they needed to be alone.

That night before crawling into their honeycomb, Dr. and Mrs. B stripped off, and threw away their shoes and clothes. No longer patchy, the shine of their black and yellow coats glinted in the moonlight.

Waking next morning, Mrs. B inspected her husband's folded wings, the thinness of his legs, and the tailored bee suit now covering the last vestige of human skin.

A fork loaded with honey-cake frozen in his right hand where she'd forced it, slumped, his face almost touched the table, Mrs. B understood he'd stay like that forever if she didn't help him.

She heard a car drive up, the doorbell ring.

Mrs. B hunkered down beside her husband without rousing him. Waited till the car drove away.

A week later, Dr. B teetered to the opening of the hive and launched himself into the air and away narrowly missing the hedge. By sundown when he still hadn't returned, Mrs. B slowly unzipped her bee suit, and blinking in the unaccustomed sunlight stepped outside to rejoin an unfamiliar world, widowed, alone.

Lonely. Lonely time. Helpless, disabled, I alone to comfort and care for him, I became a witch. Alone together 24 hours, I disassembled. Too old to stress and strain, how long could we go on.

How shall we manage. Kneeling at his feet, we wept.

Not yet legal, assisted suicide we decided was not an option.

Caring for their beloveds, did other caregivers suffer like I did? Help. We needed help. I needed help.

But I found no shoulder on which to lay my head. No advice or training on how to keep on going.

ELEANOR'S GIFT

"Poor Eleanor, she's touched," the villagers whispered whenever she passed. "Never the same since her husband died," they all agreed.

Eleanor had not spoken since that day. Gesturing hands and movements of her head sufficed. She became a master of expression. She could twist her mouth to show pleasure and disgust as skillfully as any words. Within her silence she saw things the villagers could not. Eleanor became a seer of death before it struck. A shape-shifter, whose nightly ritual gave life a purpose. The year was 1888 when her village was still as an island half a day distant by foot from their neighbor, surrounded by a sea of crops and golden haystacks. A pub, a church, a butcher, a baker, a grocer and a scattering of thatched cottages nestled about a 'green' and a duck-pond, the village was complete.

Eleanor lived in the cottage by the two hundred year-old oak-tree where Lover's Lane began.

No-one ever saw her leave. But when evening came around Eleanor slid into the night leaving her darkened cottage silent but for the occasional spit and flutter of an oil lamp burning on her bedroom windowsill, its square panes beaming stepping-stones across her patch of grass for her return, its light illuminating the oak tree on Lovers Lane, a spot where couples liked to stop to snatch a kiss and cuddle. The girls' backs pushed hard against the roughness of the bark, their up-turned faces faintly yellowed by the beam, while boys' hands fumbled at their homespun clothing.

No-one asked her where she went each night, but by putting two and two together, the villagers had long figured out it was she, Eleanor, who visited each cottage and hovel tiptoeing, tap-tapping on the window glass or doors like a stray vine dancing to the wind.

'Do you hear her?' They might question, or 'Eleanor's doing her rounds early tonight.' they might say.

The villagers had come to expect it. They listened out for her. But in the beginning when the sounds and sightings first occurred, they'd tried catching who or what it was. Tap-tap. They'd burst open their front doors finding nothing. Some nights they heard soft rustling. Some swore they'd seen the shadow of a giant bird silhouetted in the dark. Others weren't so sure. 'Just a kid in costume hoping to scarify us,' they'd re-assure.

After a storm they'd discover three-toed footprints in the snow or mud. The giant blackbird, or Eleanor, if that was she, stayed hidden.

But if, when they awoke next morning, a feather, just one purple-black plume, was found lying on the doorstep, that villager would know death was on the wing; that death would claim a member of their household within the next full cycle of the sun and moon. That someone would die abed, be struck down in his prime, or have an accident as had Eleanor's husband many years back. He'd been found stiff, face down in the village pond after a violent summer windstorm whipped every leaf from the trees snapping thick branches like they were kindling wood, and stripped the thatch from many a cottage. At first they thought his body was a fallen branch, that his widespread arms and legs were the branches' limbs. She'd begged him not to venture abroad, begged him to wait until the sky's anger abated. But no…. 'It's my duty as mayor,' he'd said, 'my duty to check all is well.' He'd fetched his jacket and stepped out.

It was the suddenness, the unexpectedness of death that

plunged Eleanor into silence. She mourned her last words to him had been unrehearsed, had not been a loving farewell.

Twelve years passed. One morning at first light, her neighbor stumbled on a willow basket heaped full with blackbird feathers on the porch step of Eleanor's cottage as she delivered a jug of milk, warm from the cow, frothy, the way she liked it. She knew then, that very instant, Eleanor was gone.

The older women wrapped her body in the black mantle they found hanging on a hook behind her kitchen door. Village men were summoned. They cut through the grass at the bottom of her garden excavating a deep rectangular hole to receive her. Four pallbearers processed from the church followed by the villagers. Each carried a black plume taken from Eleanor's basket, one plume enough for every villager yet living, one each for those whose time was not yet come. They let their plume flutter onto Eleanor's swaddled form lying in the pit. Feathered as any a blackbird, they covered her with earth.

It was a kindness, the villagers decided once the burial was over, Eleanor's way of giving them the advance notice of which she had been deprived. Eleanor's way of giving them time to say their goodbyes, to forgive and make amends for deeds done and left undone, time to don clean undergarments and stockings to meet their Maker.

A weather-worn headstone carved from wood reads,

FAREWELL SWEET BLACKBIRD.
WHO GAVE US TIME TO SING
FAREWELL

Death is much on my mind. Consumes me. The suddenness of it. When David sleeps, I lie awake listening, listening. Nothing. Not a sound can I hear. Leaping from bed I stand at his door. Shudder when at last I hear him inhale long and noisily.

David with his loss of ability. Me? Robbed of the freedom I lived, Parkinson's governs both David's life and mine forcing me to travel paths not every one of my choosing. Mother. Lover. Speech Pathologist. Painter. Sculptor. Writer. Nurse. OT, Physio therapist. Caregiver... With so much of the real me erased, so much imposed, who am I now?

I look in the mirror. See, not me, but that wild-eyed woman who took my place. I no longer exist.

THE PADDED DOOR

The young woman could wait no longer. A week widowed, her husband's ashes barely cooled, she stared at the padded door to the den her husband had never allowed her to enter.

Now, she muttered, now she'd find out what it was her husband hadn't wanted her to see. Her tortured mind traveled every avenue…girlie pictures, stolen goods, drugs, red-ribboned bound love-letters, evidence of some outlandish fetish, a shrine to his first wife maybe…

For fifteen years, hours a day, her husband stayed closeted behind the padded door.

"Just a wee peep darling…P-l-e-a-se?" She wheedled sliding her arms around his neck proffering her puckered lips.

Teasing. Threats. Anger. She thumped, pummeled his chest the way she often pummeled the door's brass-studded green leather.

His granite face cracked a smile.

"What's in there is for me to find alone."

The padded room remained a bone between them, gnawed, but unburied. Once, twice, twenty times or more, when first they married and her curiosity was at its zenith, she hovered, waited for him to emerge…lunchtime, for afternoon tea, and at six o'clock cocktail hour as the chiming of their hall clock signaled his last exit of the day.

"Boo." Hoping to surprise him, creeping up on hands and knees, she made a dive for the gap between his legs. But as a snail keeps hidden the interior of its shell-house, her husband filled the darkened portal with his form, exposed not a sliver, not a glimmer of what lay behind.

To her mind, their marriage, a second for them both, was like that door—padded. That apart, their union, though childless, cruised calmly along as normal and happy as most any marriage. They shared a marital bed, made love on Sunday mornings, fought for space in the kitchen, dined seated opposite ends of the dining room table, and occasionally played dress-up to enliven marriage's boredom. Then, he, the tinsel man bedecked in a sparkling suit, bowler hat, sported an elastic-sprung neon light-up bow tie. She, his rouged-cheeked puppet in flamingo-pink tutu flaunted black fishnet stockings. Electric blue sequins sparkling the floor and oak stair treads, marked the trail of night's frivolity, their madcap chase, the frenzied tugging, fumbling at one another's clothes to climax with each other's passion.

As well as that, on fine summer evenings, iced drink in hand, the couple loved to sit outside beside the ornamental lily pond and feed their goldfish.

Just over a week ago, before… the two of them had settled in their lawn chairs to feed the fish. And she had watched her husband kneel and feed houseflies from an empty matchbox—flies her husband collected from the window panes, some squished, some still twitching.

"Kutchi-koo. Come my beauty," he cooed to his favorite, holding a fly-treat by its wings to the water's surface. Kalahari-koo, Kamphor-koo, Kismet-koo, Korali-koo, Koroline… In turn he called each six fish by name.

As her husband knelt to part the green growth of Lily pads covering the surface, he revealed a blackness of water in the rectangular pond her eyes could not penetrate. Just like that damnable door she muttered. Laying her head against the canvas chair she stared into the sky to wipe the image from her mind with warm sunlight.

If the woman had known it was their last time feeding the fish together before finding her husband lying on his back outside his den—dead, his eyes rolled towards the padded door, perhaps her thoughts would have been more charitable. But her pent-up angry curiosity, got the better of her and though barely a week widowed, she had sprinkled his ashes to the fish.

"Now...," she gloated, "let's see what you've kept hidden all these years."

"Hello," the woman called a Handyman service.

"I want the lock removed and the hinges loosened, but do not open the door. Leave it up and closed. Understand? The door must not be opened," she instructed ignoring the workmen's arched brows, the smirks they exchanged.

Hovering, she stood over them, making sure. What lay inside was hers alone, not for sharing.

At last, they were gone. She could wait no longer. She grabbed a screwdriver, made for the still standing door. One jiggle, one push, the hinges gave, the barrier fell inward to expose her husband's island, an island no footprints but his had trod, where no breath but his had stirred the air. She hovered in the doorway, hesitant, before taking a deep breath she placed her left foot over the portal.

"Whaa....the hell? The hell, the hell?" Her howl bounced from all four walls.

Mirrors. Silvery mirrors covered all four walls and the ceiling, every surface but the sky-blue carpeted floor shimmered with mirrors. A thousand reflections mocked, stared back at herself.

Eyes darting, across the room she took in a chair, a dainty three-legged, pedestal table beneath the bottle-paned window on which lay three books. Each hard cover carried a title. Past. Present. Future. Pristine glossy pages filled all three. Scrabbling their pages, the first, the second, the third also, revealed not a letter, not a word, nor an image—not one.

Frenzied, she peered beneath the table, the chair, as if by searching she'd discover who and what he kept hidden from her these long fifteen years. It was then she noticed the table's small drawer. Unlocked, it slid open. Inside—a silver-backed beveled mirror. Snatching it, she slithered sobbing to the floor. Frantic, she turned it this way and that.

No reflection. No face. No image gazed back from the mirror glass she held before her.

So early? I was about to argue, when one after-noon around four, David announced firmly he'd like me to get him ready for bed.

I checked in later. Asleep, he hadn't stirred. Next morning, head on his pillow, he still lay as he had.

You do realize he'll never leave his bed again? The Hospice nurse dropped her bomb. Then, closing the front door behind her, she left.

Her words exploded. Took time to sink in. Collect the fragments. And when I realized what she meant, in a panic I fetched a plastic bag and threw in every single pair of his shoes. His bed-room slippers too.

I can't bear it, I sobbed seeing his clothes hang-ing closet. Then into another bag went in every shirt, pair of pants, underwear, socks and every jacket. All but his T-shirts. One of those I kept back. The new one we'd chosen together a month back but not yet worn.

Day after day he lay there in a coma, until just like that, one day he died. Visitors stopped vis-iting. Lonely, hopeless, I survived. Prayed for David's return. Some sign.

THE VISITOR

I saw him standing in the frost beneath the oak tree at the end of my lawn—a man in a blue-grey tunic. With the rising sun behind him, I thought at first David stood there. I jumped. It was then I noticed a bird perched on his left shoulder, and on his outstretched hands, two sparrows pecking at what I supposed were crumbs. Because my cottage garden abutted the village churchyard over the wall, my first thought was the ghost of a long-departed had risen from its grave to visit awhile.

Seeing my face pressed to the window-glass, he turned, smiled, and beckoned indicating I should come out to join him. I wrapped my dressing gown about me tightly and opened the door. When I reached him, I saw his feet were bare and a long white knotted cord hung tied about his waist. A thousand pins prickled up and down my spine.

"Well blow me down, the man looks like…" I pinched myself from such a silly thought.

Half smiling, the stranger nodded as if he read my mind, and handing me a torn lump of bread mimed I should hold out my hand like his. Out of nowhere, a black raven dropped from the bare branches of the nearby Elm tree, so close his wings brushed my cheeks with his feathery touch and made me flinch. He curled his talons round my forefinger for a moment, grabbed a morsel of bread from my palm, then swooped away. A little alarmed, I turned to (…I almost dared to call him by name…well, you know who…) so still, I wondered how he could support the throng of sparrows roosted along both arms. One even settled on the baldpate island of his head. Surrounded by his tonsure, it gave the appearance of a bird crouched over its nest hatching a giant egg.

When the first rabbit hopped towards him to sit at his feet followed by another and another, I was certain. The man who stood at the bottom of my garden was the saint himself. My body trembled. And with my recognition a glow ignited around his form and grew so bright I fell to my knees. Fearing I would burst like him into a fiery ball, I buried my face in the frosted grass daring to raise it only when the cold assured me I had not floated to another realm that was not earth.

My visitor was gone. His glow remained, a filtered light of beams dancing through the Elm's leafless twigs showed the sun climbing into day. Sparrows fluttering above, three rabbits at my feet, breadcrumbs gritty, damp in my palm, I knew my visitor had been real and human kindness offered to another, though but a crumb, can be as glorious as a feast.

Then covid struck. Everyone I knew isolated in their own canoe, I called my friends, they called me. Just checking, we'd say. How are you doing? Strangely, I found myself less lonely. I didn't say never, I said less lonely.

FLASH IN THE PAN

I bought a goldfish almost one week ago.

A Covid-19 reflex, I explained to my zoom classmates. The shelter's out of dogs, you see. I held a plastic bag before the computer screen to show my fish alive and swimming.

In exchange for eleven dollars and sixty cents, a bubble-wrapped glass bowl, green plastic sprig of water-weed, and a shaker of fish food arrived courtesy of Fed-EX Overnight Delivery.

A welcome change from TV, for five whole evenings, first thing after class, I sat absorbed before its bowl bonding with my new pet.

Kutchi-koo, dear Thingy, I called in a high-pitched fish-friendly tone. Mummy's here.

Gold and orange, round it sped snapping at each crumb I sprinkled.

Come play my beauty. I tapped its glass. Not once did Thingy blow me a bubble-kiss or make eye contact.

Day six. That's it. I hissed. Lucky for you I don't have a cat.

I emptied the bowl down the toilet and flushed, poured myself a glass of Burgundy red, and flipped on my favorite television station.

*C*ovid gave me the gift of time. The hours quarantined alone to reminisce and to relive the trajectory of my life. Time to cry and mourn. Time to laugh and time to, yes, cringe as I revisit things I'd rather forget.

Spain. Ah Spain. Who would I be but for those eleven summers in Spain? I devoured the black and white images I'd captured. The villagers, my children, the harvest's cycle… could that have really been fifty years ago? A new book emerged. Three years flashed by. Too quickly in fact.

WHEN COWS WORE SHOES

Set in a mountain village of the Picos de Europa, Northern Spain, during the last years of Franco's reign, when cows really did wear shoes and people threshed grain riding wooden sledges, a method first mentioned two thousand years ago, the book records way of life we can only dream of today. Romanticized maybe, harshly honest, eleven summers through the eyes of an English family describes a time when people had no use for machines or money until its bumpy transition into the twentieth century, when porn, potatoes, plumbing changed everything. Fiestas, Harvest, Threshing, stories of camp life and buried wine, lie hidden within these pages.

WIDOW. I tick the space under Marital Status. Still hate the label.

Five years have passed since I last saw David. I glimpse him in dreams sometimes. And startle at his voice.

Go for it, Liz, I hear.

And so, I do. India, France, England, Japan, Spain, Mexico of course, and although I've begun traveling again with friends and family, I don't understand the merry part of Merry Widow, for though I'd describe myself as content, merry I am not.

MERRY WIDOW

Breaking records, the thermometer fluctuated between 95 and 100 degrees. Not just for a day. I had endured living in a furnace for three weeks already. My feet and ankles swollen tree trunks, I kicked off my sandals at the front door. Inside, I tugged at my ring finger where the gold pinched tight. It hurt. Water. I needed water. I ran to the kitchen. After downing two full glasses I held my hand beneath the cold tap till my finger shrank enough for me to slip my wedding and engagement rings off never thinking of the signal its nakedness broadcast.

I stared at the band of white flesh unseen since my first marriage sixty years ago. Rubbed life back into the indent marking the rings' symbolic grip. Wiggled my fingers. Unfettered. Free. Was my subconscious telling me something? Letting me know I was ready? Ready for what? That an accident of heat made me rip them off, I tossed the thought aside.

Placing the two rings on the coffee table, I stacked one on top of the other within reach. Admired their delicate design. Just in case… I thought. But I never missed their tightness, the comfort they brought me in time of stress. Waiting for a no-show, for example, or, watching or hearing something unsettling. Times like those, then round and round, I'd twist them. Calmed me right down.

I turned off the TV, undressed for bed and slept the sleep of an angel. Next morning there on the coffee table where I'd left them, they sparkled. Surprised, I scooped them up and hid them in the safety of my junk jewelry drawer. Nobody would find them there. Forgot I ever wore them.

Almost a month now, they've stayed there. Off my finger.

Needing to see a dentist, (mine is in Mexico) and as a good excuse to escape the heatwave and cool off in the ocean, I flew to Puerto Vallarta. No David, no girlfriend to accomapny me, my first holiday alone.

What? You're going on your own? Friends look me up and down. Not saying, but clearly thinking, what, old lady, traveling by yourself at your age?

I've booked wheel chair assistance, I parry, suddenly defensive.

Come cocktail hour, the hour when the sun trembles for a moment low in the sky, before it takes the plunge and sinks from my sight below the horizon, I watch a lone pelican gathering his treasures of plankton and small fish from the light-tinged waves. I sigh. Observe how couples move closer, touch heads at sunset. Miss my David. Cheers sweetheart, I toast, lift my glass. Can't believe I've been a widow five years. Some days whisk by so fast I lose track, and have to check my cell phone to tell me today's Thursday, fool, not Tuesday. Then there are those other days, those long first years of widowhood, when my world stopped spinning and I became a sloth.

Solitude and I are friends now. Surprisingly, I didn't mind eating in a restaurant on my own. Or swimming. Or walking on the sand. David and I were never much for touchy-touchy anyway, so I'm just fine. Down in the resort restaurant on the seafront, I almost laughed out loud as a plate of tuna, not the snapper I ordered is placed before me.

Order what you like, take what you are given. David's favorite dictum slides into my mind.

Although cartwheels are not happening, and skippy-skippy is not how I'd describe my state, this un-merry widow smiles content. Content. I can live with content, but jolly? That's a feeling

I realize I am missing. I strain to catch what set the group at the next table to mine laughing. Unabashed, open-mouthed, really laughing. I haven't laughed like that for who knows how many years. Yes I do miss laughter, I do miss jolly.

But there is a shift. In my people watching. It's not intentional, but I find I am scanning the resort checking men out. Muscles. Body tattoos. Bronze torsos. Judging, of course and for the worse, mostly. Thank God, I'm not hitched to him. I glance briefly at the unhealthy food heaped on his plate, the way he eats, what he wears, guess at his political affiliation, how he spends his evenings, and shudder picturing his naked body hovering over his wife... On and on. Not nice of me, I know. It's a family resort, no singles that I can see. Clearly no-one wants to talk to the old bat I am.

"Could you take a photo of me, please?" I ask a concierge handing her my cell phone.

I study the photo. Whoa? A woman, me, in a yellow and navy floral Hawaiian knee-length shorts, and black skin-hugging shoestring top. Sunglasses of course. Not half bad, well, for my age. So that's what I look like now. Sexy, even though I say so myself. Vanity, vanity... I swing my beach bag and walk a little straighter after that.

Back in New Mexico, half a year later, my feet are itchy. I had to get away again.

Japan, I decide. Like a traveling companion? A girlfriend asks. More fun with two. I jump at her offer. One month? We agree, and I get to planning. Every hotel must have an Onsen, one of our only stipulations. I mug up on a few necessary phrases in Japanese. Tore-wa doku des ka? I practiced. Yup, we'd need that one to find the toilet.

I loved Onsens, my daily soak up to my neck in their natural hot waters. No better way to begin the day. Way north of Tokyo we stayed five days near the snow monkeys' swimming holes in a mountain village boasting nine onsens on the main street alone. Though our modest hotel didn't have its own, each evening the hotel drove us to bathe in a different onsen to experience a variety of settings…from almost a hole in the ground to the landscaped soaking pool of a luxurious hotel set in a bamboo grove with artistically placed rocks.

The moon was up casting an intricate weave of shadow bamboo leaves on the water. Moving like lizards from rock to rock, my friend Jennifer and I soaked in the steaming mineral springs for as long as our bodies could stand.

Still dressed in my kimono, my kimono and nothing else, waiting for her and the rest of our group to go back to our hotel, I stood alone on the empty landing. And while I waited, noticed a hanging string of pastel colored origami paper birds. As I bent to look more closely, a door swung open right beside me making me jump.

A Japanese man emerged. "Konban-wa, Good evening," he bowed startled to find me outside his room.

"Konban-wa," I returned, sort of bending at the waist as I knew women were expected to do. Ah good, I thought, I'll ask him the significance of the many strings of birds I'd seen in Japan.

"Shimimasen. Excuse me, Sir," I bowed slightly again, and pointing to the birds queried, "Please, can you explain their meaning to me?"

In answer, the most beautiful birdsong trilled from his puckered lips.

My eyes opened wide and I looked at him, really looked for the first time.

Distinguished. Elegant, yes, those adjectives perfectly describe him. My height, an inch taller maybe, about my age, his grey hair groomed and neatly trimmed, grey kimono tightly wrapped covering his nakedness, I sank into the grey-blueness of his eyes. Kindly. Intelligent. Sensitive, his eyes flashed.

Though not as musical, nor able to create the intricate cadences and flow of his magical notes, I responded with whistled psalms of my own. Call and response. Call and response. A courtship. A lovebird's declaration passed between us.

We let the silence that followed hang a moment. Then bowing to one another looked deep into each other's eyes.

"Would you do me the honor, ma'am, of joining me for dinner?" He bowed.

"It would have been my honor to accept, Sir, and I thank you. Sadly, I am with another group from a different hotel and am obligated to refuse."

A last exchange of bows, one last look of longing, and my handsome suitor was gone.

Neither of us noticed Jennifer. That she had finished dressing some time back and stood beside us.

"Wow. Sorry to interrupt. Talk about chemistry," she exclaimed. "I thought for a moment I'd lost you and I'd be spending the rest of the holiday on my own."

"Well actually I…" I didn't finish the sentence. Rubbing my finger where my wedding band used to be, I avoided her gaze, glad she couldn't see the scenes playing in my mind.

$\mathcal{P}$OSSIBILITIES

My first solo trip over, my wedding band removed,
I discovered that I was still alive and nothing
bad had happened while living outside my shell.
There was nothing I couldn't do. (Well, except
scratch my own back perhaps)

Like Barbie in the movie, I no longer need mans',
nor anyone's approval, to slop around bra-free
in sweatpants, or to fancy-up and take myself
out to a sushi dinner and concert. The Long,
the Short and the Tall complete, I'm off now to
England, and to the South of France to immerse
myself in a two-week residential French Course,
and to spend time with my family.

Then what?

I made a list of possibilities. Of coulds.

I could survive alone anywhere I chose. I don't
need a partner but acknowledge it is possible I
could fall in love again.

I could stay home, disconnect the phone and tune into the birdsong trilling outside my dining room window. Hmm. That sounded nice.

I could…

I could…

I could…

I faced another void. To jump this way or that, or not jump at all?

Idly watching a television talent show the other evening, my attention was caught by an escape artist writhing to escape his chains and leather casing. All at once bounding free, he stared into the camera waving to his unseen audience. Young and fit, victorious, I swore the escape art-ist stared at me, just as the Butterfly Messenger had beamed his message into the screen more than forty years before.

TWO MAGIC WORDS

the magician holds a card before me
are these the word you wrote he asks
this one
this
I shake my head
spreads a fan of five and twenty images
jokers, diamonds, kings and queens
choose any one you like he leers
pushes mine into the pack
but the cards are glued
stuck
the magician laughs at my futile struggle
that night as I prepare for bed
discover words scrawled on a card
between the cotton folds of my nightie
live now

ACKNOWLEDGMENTS

Donna. Thank-you. Thank-you. First and foremost, co-editor, brilliant cover and book designer, Donna comes to mind. She's worked patiently beside me for almost ten years to date. And, thanks to her have five books published.

I thank my mother for supporting me until my Green Card arrived allowing me to stay and become a dual citizen of America.

I thank America for helping me grow. I thank my adopted country for giving me these stories and the opportunity to write them.

ALSO BY E.P. ROSE

Poet Under A Soldier's Hat

Ditty Dotty Ditties

portraits : poems

The Perfect Servant... nope

When Cows Wore Shoes